SKEWERED PERSPECTIVE

A PARKER PHOTOGRAPHY COZY MYSTERY

SUZANNE BOLDEN

CONTENTS

CHAPTER ONE

My fingers wrapped around my hot coffee mug for warmth against a chill in the morning air. The village green, still glistening with morning dew, spread out before me. I loved this little balcony off my second-story apartment to sit on and enjoy watching Harmony wake up.

Our local weatherman's forecast was for scattered clouds and highs in the mid-70s today. Perfect! I was grateful that there was no rain forecast for today or Sunday, because this was the Taste of Harmony's opening day.

Yesterday afternoon, I had watched the vendors hustle to set up their booths. They staked tents out, towed in wagons with pickups, and backed food trucks into position. The center stage's audio system was ready for the scheduled performances. My Aunt Ruth and her friends from Shady Pines Retirement Village had the table and chairs set up for selling tickets. Our committee decided to allow alcohol because Orin at the Stone Mill Brewery had created a beer just for the Taste of Harmony, Sweet Harmony Shandy. Aunt Ruth's ticket selling group was also tasked with verifying ages of anyone wanting alcohol. After confirming their age, they would lock a neon green band on their wrist.

The Harbor Dogs food stand, on the edge of the village green near the path to the marina, was owned by my friend Val's son, Travis. Early morning fishermen enjoyed grabbing a breakfast sandwich and hot coffee on their way to the marina. During winter, their hours corresponded with the opening of the skating rink on the green, and they served delicious marshmallow-laden hot chocolate.

It had surprised me when Val told us she'd be helping run the Harbor Dogs during the Taste. "Do you think you'll get much business? I mean, there will be so many other food choices."

Val's response had been, "Ah, Jackie. You've got to think outside your box as a single woman. Kids. There will be kids! And a fresh cold gazpacho from Timber Grill or pickled vegetables from Patti's Country Kitchen Catering might not entice the littles. They will grumble and whine to mom and dad. But a good hot dog? Or chicken tenders? Or a little cheese pizza? We're going to be busy. I guarantee it."

I watched as Val raised the hinged panel that covered the open counter of the hot dog stand this morning. She locked in the braces to hold it up, forming a little roof. Her grandsons Tony and Thad finished hanging a special sign. I hoped it would be a great day financially for the boys. They were good kids. Hard workers.

From here I also watched as Claude, our local barber, along with his wife Vivian, pushed a clumsy, wheeled serving cart across the village green's bumpy path. They'd convinced a recalcitrant Dolly to set up a booth for her diner. Dolly's Diner was directly across from the edge of the village green, so Claude had suggested a spot on the far side of the green for more exposure. I hoped Dolly would join them because not only was her food abundant with home-cooked deliciousness, but she herself was a character and a draw for customers.

I had done little work for the committee after finishing up marketing photographs weeks ago. But for today and tomorrow, they assigned me to prowl the grounds, watching for underage drinkers trying to sneak a beer. I would have eyes out for those neon green wristbands whenever I saw a plastic drink cup raised to someone's lips.

Of our dozen restaurants, four paid the extra fee required to serve alcohol. I thought it best if they were near each other, which meant they all were setup near the river and walking path because Miguel, owner of Miguel's Brazilian Steakhouse, explained the smoke from the spit-roasted meat might annoy guests. We used his suggestion that the steakhouse tents be set up where winds sent the smoke out over the river. The Stone Mill featured their Sweet Harmony Shandy, the Mexican food truck offered margaritas, and the Wildwood Supper Club served their classic old-fashioned. Miguel served the Brazilian national cocktail, caipirinha, a drink made by mixing lime and fruit, then adding cachaca, a sugarcane-based liquor.

All in all, things were right on track for opening at eleven. The Taste of Harmony would draw people from the surrounding area but also tourists, many of whom had summer places at The Hills Resort on the western edge of Harmony.

It looked to be a good day. Harmony was ready.

I finished up my coffee, showered, and prepared for the day ahead. Comfortable walking shoes were a must, as were my sunglasses. The weatherman's forecast of light cloud cover might be wrong. So far there was full sunshine without a cloud in sight.

The gallery downstairs from my apartment was quiet. Todd would open the Parker Photography Studio today, but first he would join me and my Chicago friends for breakfast at Dolly's Diner. He knew Celeste and Felicia from his time in Chicago and looked forward to catching up with them.

I took a moment to look at my front window displays. One window held prints of photographs I'd done on my travels around the world. I worked hard to make myself a well-known and respected photographer. It had been my manager Mandy's suggestion that we do this. She argued that new tourists in town for the food festival might recognize my work and be pleased to know it had found a permanent place here.

I agreed with her, but only if the other window showcased Mandy's contribution to our business. She'd carefully chosen works from her recent class, which focused on the impact of perspective in photography. Her classes all included basics of framing, which was becoming a lucrative side job for her. The class photographs she chose for display were all beautifully framed.

Parker Photography put on an eye-catching display for these special days.

CHAPTER TWO

The smells of bacon and coffee hit me as I entered Dolly's Diner. I was welcomed with hugs all around. Todd slid across the booth to make room for me.

"Sorry we missed meeting up with you at the Wildwood last night. Whew, what a traffic mess leaving Chicago. Summer tourists getting out-of-town time is here." Celeste looked as stylish as ever in her denim jacket, caramel t-shirt, and white jeans. She held up her palm. "I know what you're thinking, Jackie, so I won't make you ask. Yes, I've had some recent Botox treatments."

"Hey, I wasn't even going to ask! I was just admiring how your youthful beauty never fades. Never a thought it wasn't natural."

"Right. Sure. You with your mantra of welcoming old age as it comes," Celeste teased. "You wear it well. Me, I'll go with working on improving myself. Whether by using Botox or dating younger men for their invigorating youthful energy."

Todd's mouth formed an exaggerated O. "Well, thanks for letting me know that. I would have offered myself. Willingly."

"Thank you, Todd, but I have a cutoff point. And someone young enough to be my son is it! But I saw a few likely candidates here during my last visit, and I may be on the prowl during this food fest."

I welcomed Dolly arriving with my coffee. "I watched Claude and Vivian get your booth all set up. Are you excited to let the world in on the delicious food you have here?"

With a snort Dolly said, "Nope, I'm not. But it's too late to back out now."

Her gruff dismissal of the day's activities didn't fool me. The small vases holding fresh wildflowers on the tables were a sign she'd stepped it up inside the diner. Val let me know she'd come to the Cut-N-Curl for a new hairdo this week. More proof that she was just a tiny bit excited.

"I think it might surprise you at how well your diner

food does. By the way, I love that new shade of lipstick on you," I said.

"Yeah right," Dolly mumbled. "It's a lot of bother to set all that up when my diner is open just a few feet away. Go figure. Now, what can I get for you all?"

"I like your new lipstick too. Felicia, why don't you go first? I'm not decided yet," Todd said, raising a hand to his brow. "But I must eat a big breakfast because I'm stuck inside all day at the studio."

"Jackie, what kind of slave driver are you?" Felicia said before ordering an English muffin.

"Wow! Don't stuff yourself," I teased. "I'm going to order a ham and two eggs over-easy breakfast, Dolly. I'll be working all day too."

"Doing what?" Celeste asked.

"Checking for underage drinkers," I said. "Patrolling the grounds round and round and round. What I'll find, I'm not sure. I would think that sort of thing wouldn't happen until later when the band starts up. I chose the hopefully peaceful day shift. Are you two going up and playing a round of golf at the Driftless Course while you're here this weekend?"

"Look, while you all are making social plans, can I get the rest of the orders?" Dolly said, tapping her pencil on her order pad.

Celeste placed her order. "Now, back to golf. Yes, we are, and we wish you could have joined us."

"I'm so rusty, but I'm planning on starting back in on the game. I've met some women who have homes at The Hills Resort, and one of them is going to give me some pointers on Monday."

"The Real Housewives of the Hills?" Todd asked. "Now that's an interesting bunch."

I almost gagged on my coffee. "Where did you get that name?"

"They call themselves that. You've never heard of it? I first heard it when Mandy had them in our studio for a class. They tease each other constantly about it."

"It has a certain fitting ring to it," I said. "I'll confess I've never watched one of those Real Housewives shows, but I've seen promotional trailers. But you guys should see the work they've done under Mandy's tutelage."

Todd nodded. "That's right. Our current front window display is from their class. Check it out. It's pretty cool. The shots involve the use of perspective."

"Like when someone looks like they're holding up the sun?" Felicia asked.

"Yeah, Phoebe did one like that. That style is called forced perspective photography," Todd said.

"Well, listen to you, knowing all that lingo," Felicia teased.

"But seriously, it's the idea of things aren't what they seem. I saw a kid who used miniature classic car models and staged them against backgrounds, making them appear full size. Really amazing."

"Junene did a linear perspective," I said. "She shot tall buildings aiming up at them. Mandy said she found a spot where she could lie down right on the street to take them."

"Sounds like you're lucky you found Mandy to work with you," Celeste said.

"Hey! Jackie's lucky she found me too," Todd interjected.

"Of course, my dear Todd. But that meant she also stole you from us. You haven't been back to Chicago since your Christmas shopping spree. We miss you, honey. Are you going small town on us?"

"Hold on. I flew out of O'Hare in February. Remember, we met for dinner?"

"Late lunch." Celeste waved her hand dismissively. "I can barely remember those twenty-two minutes at an airport restaurant. And you, Todd, were seriously distracted. Your mind was on that Alli girl you were meeting in California."

Todd blushed.

I saved him. "Yes, I am lucky to have both of them

working with me. And I'm blessed that Mandy will be my daughter-in-law."

You could have heard a pin drop before Celeste and Felicia both shrieked. "What? That handsome hunk with Sam Elliott's voice? When? Where?"

"We'll talk later at the Taste. Let's all plan on meeting around five? You should be done with your golf, and I'll be done with my committee duties."

"Sounds great. And didn't you mention a band will be playing?" Felicia said. "I like the sound of that. No rap or heavy metal, I hope."

"Cover band for the best of the decades songs," Todd said. "I'll be there too. But right now, back to opening up the studio. See you guys later."

Celeste checked her watch. "We should hit the road too. We still have to pick up our clubs back at Kay's. That's such a lovely B&B. But maybe next time we come, you'll be moved in with Scott, and we can invite ourselves to stay with you."

"Hey, are you planning on keeping your loft in Chicago?" Felicia stood and grabbed our check. "I sure hope so."

"It's something we're thinking about," I said. "I'm not sure. But we're not getting married until later this year. I'm thinking of a Christmas wedding. The village is so beautiful then."

"And you're staying in that little apartment until then? Come on, Jackie, this is the 21st century."

"I love my little apartment."

"Of course you do, but I loved those snapshots you sent from Scott's deck. What a view! It's not Lake Michigan, but still ranks up there," Celeste said, giving me a wink and waving goodbye. "And there are a lot of long, cold months before Christmas. Catch you later."

CHAPTER THREE

My first stop at the Taste was to check in with Aunt Ruth at the ticket sales table.

"I thought you were going to bring Libby to sit with us," Dorothy said as I approached the table.

Bracing her feet solidly on the ground, Dorothy used her tall sturdy frame to lift one side of the ticket table while Betty shoved a piece of folded cardboard under the table's leg. Eunice's arm flew out across the table's contents, which were threatening to slide over the edge. Aunt Ruth reached for the metal money box, snatching it up before it slid against Eunice's arm. Dorothy let the table drop back down and tried rocking the long wooden beast back and forth. "She's steady now."

"All this because of a little wobbling? Sometimes I

swear you are the most persnickety person I've ever met," Eunice said.

Betty scolded Eunice for her crotchety remark. "It was bothering me too. We'll have pennies rolling off the table all day long if it remains askew because of a dimple in the ground."

I had to hold back a smile at Eunice's eye roll and her loud, dramatic sigh. "There are no pennies in our cash box to roll off our lovely ticket table. And don't go personifying the ground, giving it dimples. Dimples are what I have on my thighs. The table was a little cockeyed, is all."

Dorothy's eyelids dropped to half-mast as her shoulders drooped. "It's going to be a long day," she said to me. "Now back to Libby."

"I was going to bring her, but I left her in the shop with Todd. I wasn't sure if she'd be in the way here."

"That little cute pup? No bother at all," Aunt Ruth said. "Maybe I'll go over later and get her."

"If you're sure. I know she'd like to be outside. Are you all set to open?"

"I think so," Betty said. "Just a couple of final touches to take care of."

"Kim came gallivanting over with a big plastic tub of her business cards for us to pass out with ticket purchases. Can you believe that? I put the kibosh on that."

"Eunice, it was a small holder of cards she wanted to sit at the edge of the table," Betty said. "I don't see the problem with it. She's such a nice gal and shows so much support for our community."

"Yeah sure. Then when the hardware store wants to put their cards out, what'll we do? Or if the dentist brings over some of his stupid tooth-shaped ones he uses for appointment reminders? Or the dog groomer and her ugly doggie bone ones? First one, then the entire table would be full. Nope. No way."

Aunt Ruth's shoulders popped up, and she gave me her silly little grin. "We're fine here, Jackie. Elmer and Harry are over at Murphy's getting us a coffee. What will you be doing today?"

"I'm tasked with mingling among the crowd, watching for any signs of trouble."

"Trouble. Goodness, what are you expecting? Is there a threat of some sort? A terrorist threat?" Betty's wide-eyed, alarmed expression caused Eunice to burst out laughing.

"Betty. Sweet Betty. We are in a tiny river town in southwest Wisconsin. We don't get terrorist threats. By trouble, Jackie might mean underage drinkers."

"Oh, that's a relief. You had me worried. Is she right?"

I nodded. "Yes, Betty. No terrorists. No murderers. No crazies."

"Well, that's a relief," Betty said. "I'm excited about the village improvements these funds will go towards. Things like road improvements. We are getting so many more vehicles creating wear and tear on our roads. Hopefully, the tourists and summer people will participate big time in our celebration of flavors from Harmony and beyond!"

Elmer and Harry brought extra coffee, and I grabbed one, then excused myself to check on any issues that might need attending to.

Stu Walters was up ahead at the Asian Fusion restaurant from Greensville. Their request to join us here, as we didn't even have a basic carryout Chinese restaurant, had excited me. That was one thing I missed about living in a big city, a wide choice in restaurants. Should I give up my loft? Scott and I enjoyed going there on the occasional weekend to catch dinner and a play, or stroll on the Lake Michigan beaches. Then hitting up a museum or maybe the Shedd Aquarium. But there are always hotels for us to stay at if I decide to sell. A big decision to make, but it can wait.

I reintroduced myself to the Asian owner. "Remember, I came to take photographs of your dishes for our event marketing purposes?"

"Ah yes. The weather is looking like it will be very nice for the weekend," the slender, dark-haired woman said. "We are happy to be a part of your Taste of Harmony. I think it's a wonderful way to meet our neighbors and introduce my restaurant to your community. I was just giving Mr. Walters some information about us for your newspaper."

"I'll let you continue your discussion. Will you and Kim be around tonight?" I asked Stu, before stepping away. "A bunch of us are gathering to listen to the band."

"We are. Kim is planning on dancing the night away."

Grace Murphy's small setup for her bakery and coffee shop was directly across the street from their storefront.

"Morning Jackie," Grace greeted me. "Quite the event for our community." She had set up donuts and muffins in attractive towers under large glass domes. A bouquet with a sign designating it was from The Flower Girl added vivid color to the display.

That reminded me I wanted to ask Kate, owner of The Flower Girl, if she'd like to do a project together. I'd been enjoying shooting micro views of wildflowers on my walks and I wanted to create an exhibit of them. Maybe Kate would like to promote her flower shop by putting floral arrangements in my studio for it. Mandy was already designing note cards using the extreme wildflower closeups for sale in our online store.

"Lot of work has been put in to make this happen. Fingers crossed it goes off without a hitch. I'm glad you did your own booth too."

"It was Dermot's idea. He said we owed it to the other food places to take part in this, along with them. He's planning on sitting here manning our spot with his brother, who's in town for a few days."

"Chief Murphy is here? Oh gosh, I haven't seen him since I was a kid."

"Former Chief Murphy," Grace said. "And I think he would scold you and tell you to call him Paddy now that you're all grownup."

"I will come by later to say hi. It feels odd calling him Paddy after only knowing him as Chief Murphy," I said.

Grace offered me a maple-frosted donut, my favorite, but I took a pass on it. "I'm planning on nibbling and sampling my way through the afternoon."

"Yoo-hoo. Jackie! Oh, Jackie!"

"Kim's in her element," Grace said. "But wearing white to a food tasting event? Not me. I'd be sure to spill or drip on myself."

Kim hurried toward us. "Isn't this exciting? I'm all aflutter with thinking of how this will really put us on the map. I know the Harmony Museum and Nature

Center was our first big draw. Then the Driftless Golf Course and all the building going on up there in The Hills Resort. But my goodness, this is the icing on our cake. We are blossoming into the place to see and be seen!"

"Don't forget the Antique Market," I said.

"How could I? That was a huge draw as well. Hey, I heard Sophia will be back in town. I haven't seen her since the Antique Market. Is she coming to congratulate her brother on your engagement?"

"She doesn't know yet. I want to surprise her. Besides, she loves visiting us here a few times a year, and she was overdue."

"When is the big day? I'm so excited for you two. I hope your marriage is as happy as mine and Stu's," Kim said, turning to reach down and flick a small piece of something off her white slacks. "Ooh, hope that doesn't stain. Probably just dust. I was at the empty retail space next to Murphy's. What a relief to get that place leased again for you and Dermot."

"We were a little worried after the children's clothing store went out," Grace said. "But we knew you'd be on it, Kim. And what a perfect tenant you found for us."

"Who's going in there?" I asked.

That was a perfect segue for Kim to start another long conversation. "You didn't know? One of our own dear librarians has leased it. I can't believe the money she's saved up for her dream. And now it's coming true! All with my suggestion and help as a realtor and part-time designer. I've been on the real estate prowl since she shared her dream with me. I'm just the person to make dreams come true."

Focus. I tried to send mind vibes to Kim, but it wasn't working, so I just interrupted and asked her which librarian and what dream?

"Ginger. The cute librarian with the cheery smile. Her dream has always been to own a bookstore. Now it's coming true."

"That's exciting. I wish her much good luck. Retail can be tough."

"See, there you are Jackie. My job requires me to have visions and implement them. Of course, she's going to do a complete rehab in the interior. Can't you just picture it? We believe there's a fireplace that was covered over. Ginger wants to open that back up and have welcoming fires for the winter months. And Grace, tell Jackie what your part in this all is."

"Since we own both spaces, we're seeing about opening the wall between our coffee shop and the future Book Nook, or whatever Ginger names it. We think that both businesses operating with that flow between them would be perfect. Rainy days and winter cold, we've got you covered. Plus, the way the building is shaped, we can expand outdoor seating as well for nice days like this."

"Just like in the big bookstores in the city," Kim added.

"Well now, that is good news! Congratulations, Kim. You are one top-notch citizen of Harmony. And you look as stunning as ever. That pale blue shirt is beautiful on you. But I need to keep going and checking on things. Only an hour until the Taste officially opens."

CHAPTER FOUR

June is Dairy Month in Wisconsin, and there are lots of events to celebrate. From breakfasts sponsored by farmer's cooperatives to dairy farms opening up for tours. Sally's locally famous Collins Cheese was often a sponsor of these events, along with the slow-pitch softball teams. She was present at little league games and the small rodeos that came through, busy making up her deep-fried cheese curds, but this event was a chance to highlight her offerings to the tourists coming into town from Illinois and Iowa. This would be her first introduction to a broader audience. She gave a big wave to me as I made my way around the perimeter of the village green where the food booths were set up.

As I was passing Dolly's Diner spot, Claude called

out. I had to admire the effort they put into the tent. A red and white checkered scene greeted customers. It had the traditional small diner feel with the old-style condiment and napkin holders. Red paper serving plates and blue plastic utensils continued the theme. The menu sign hanging at the front of the tent clearly spelled out the food choices and how many tickets were required for each one. Vivian wore a ruffled checkered apron and Claude a white shirt with a red bow tie and suspenders.

"Don't you two look cute!"

"We're trying," Claude said. "Could you quick take a photo of us before everyone shows up? I want to frame it and put it up in my barbershop."

"Of course, I'd be happy to. I hope everyone does this and posts on social media."

Claude adjusted his bow tie. "Don't count on us for that. But I'll get one of our grandkids to do it."

"If we don't totally embarrass them with all this," Vivian chuckled.

Stu Walters saw us and came hurrying over. He was a bit out of breath when he stopped. "Please let me take this. I want to post it in our online paper edition. Why don't you get in there with them, Jackie?"

"Oh no. Just get them. I'll take one with Claude's phone for now while you can take one for your paper," I said.

Stu knew that having shots of the Taste festivities during the day would be good, but he liked the idea of each vendor having one taken in front of their booth before the people started arriving. I snapped one of Claude and Vivian proudly standing in front of the Dolly's Diner tent, then stepped away to let Stu take over.

The next restaurant was the Brazilian steakhouse. I stopped to ask if they had questions, but mostly because I was nosy. It was clear they'd done this many times. Cuts of meat, run through with large skewers, were being rotated slowly over burning briquettes. The drippings sent flames shooting up with a pleasing sizzle. Enticing smokey scents wafting out would draw a large crowd.

"Can I help you?" A handsome, dark-eyed Latin man appeared at my side.

A little flustered, I hesitated a beat, and the corners of his mouth stretched out ever so slightly. With a questioning tilt of his head, he said, "Perhaps you are hungry. Would you enjoy a sample of rotisserie-grilled beef? Yes?"

"No. I mean, not right now. Ah, later though."

"Very well. I will look for you to come by again." He extended his hand. "I'm Miguel, owner of Miguel's Brazilian Steakhouse. And you are?"

"Jackie Parker. I'm on the committee running this event. I wanted to see if everything was working out for you. Is there anything I can do for you?" Oh jeez, that was awkward.

"Well, young lady…," Miguel had spoken again when we were interrupted by Pierre, the manager and chef of the Timbers Grill in The Hills Resort.

Pierre appeared miffed. "I wish to lodge a complaint on the locations of these tents. Who came up with this arrangement? I believe I was one of the first businesses to commit to this event and I thought that meant I would get first pick of locations."

Miguel forced a smile. "Excuse me, sir, but I was speaking to Ms. Parker. Perhaps you could wait a moment. She was asking if I had questions for her. I believe she's been asking everyone and I'm sure she will get to your site soon."

"I'm here now," Pierre snapped.

Miguel turned and took my elbow, gently leading me behind the counter area and toward the rear where the meat was roasting.

"I'd like you to see how we set up our operation here," Miguel said. "We are trying our best to keep the smoke wafting…"

"Jacqueline, I demand an explanation."

I couldn't believe it, but Pierre had followed us! At

least Miguel had the wisdom to take this discussion to the back, where it would not be witnessed by guests arriving to enjoy the Taste of Harmony.

"Sir, I must insist you wait out front. As you can see, we've roped off our area, so no one enters by mistake and risks getting a burn from the hot coals or getting speared by one of our sharp skewers." To emphasize his point, Miguel grabbed a serving skewer from the rack and pointed it at Pierre. It must have been four feet long and looked like something a knight would use in battle.

Pierre reactively stepped back, almost tripping, but caught himself by putting his hand down on a table that was near the roasting area. He quickly pulled it off the heat, and I smelled the singe. But it wasn't from his skin burning, it was from a bandage on his hand. He shook it and blew on it. What on earth was happening here?

"Do you now see what your rudeness has accomplished? You are a lucky man that your hand was bandaged, or you would have required first aid. Now please leave and let me finish my conversation with Ms. Parker. She will be along to answer your questions when we are finished here. Is that correct, *mi preciosa?*"

Pierre glared at Miguel before spinning on his heel and pushing aside a worker. He stomped out of the area, his head held high.

"I hope I didn't make trouble for you, but I could not tolerate such rudeness."

I thought about my first impression of Pierre when Mandy and I went to shoot the marketing photographs of his food. He seemed pleasant, even offering Mandy side work to take photographs to use in his menus and on social media.

"I'm surprised by Pierre's behavior. It's not like him to act like that," I said.

"I'm not. Our paths have crossed before and I suspect he has a bit of jealousy in him. For instance, Pierre is not his given name. It's Peter. The Pierre sounds more like a proper French chef, don't you agree? In my humble opinion, he puts on airs. A man who would use a derivative in such a manner is to be questioned in other dealings." Miguel shrugged. "But enough of all that. On with the show. We must begin serving shortly."

"Best of luck to you today," I said.

Miguel laughed and reached for my hand to kiss it. "I wish you much success today as well."

CHAPTER FIVE

Continuing my way around the circle of restaurants, I realized I wouldn't get to the Timbers Grill tent for a few more minutes, so I picked up my pace. Orin from the Stone Mill brewery was next.

He beamed. "It feels wonderful to be out here. I've never been part of one of these. Your committee has done a terrific job. Thanks for checking on us. We're ready to go!"

The Mexican restaurant from Greensville had a cute food truck and, like Miguel, were old hands at setting up for crowds. Wildwood, our local supper club, was the final booth serving liquor. They were okay, except for requesting another power cord. I promised someone would be over with it shortly.

The Riverview Terrace Cafe, located in the visitor center for Frank Lloyd Wright's Taliesin, featured locally sourced and sustainable ingredients. Mark Peters, Taliesin's director, was helping the restaurant staff out. Somehow, they had created a false front in the Prairie style of Taliesin for their booth.

"Wow Mark, this is really eye-catching. Great job!"

"Nice to see you, Jackie. I appreciated the lovely photograph you sent over to me at Christmas. The memories of our time at Taliesin were delightful."

"Except for finding the body at the base of the Romeo and Juliet Tower," I said.

"Except for that. What a tragedy. Tara was such a sweet young woman."

"She certainly was. I'll continue on along now. Hope all goes well today."

I came to Timber Grill. Taking a deep breath, I approached Pierre, who was directing staff regarding portion sizes.

"Pierre, sorry to hear you're upset about your location."

"Jackie, I owe you an apology for my rudeness. It's just that Miguel rubs me wrong. He's making such a big show, what with that prime location and two spots, no less."

"He requested and paid for two booth spots. We moved him to that location specifically because the prevailing winds would blow his smoke out over the river instead of into the crowds. Another determining factor for locations was that anyone serving liquor be in the same area, making it easier to monitor. If you'd planned on providing such beverages, you would have been in the group over there."

"Understood. Management didn't feel alcohol was warranted. And who am I but the lowly head chef?"

"I thought you were a manager too."

"In some areas I am." He cleared his throat. "Well, I'd best crack the whip here as we open in a few minutes." He glanced at his watch, which reminded me of his injury. He was now wearing a plastic glove over the bandage.

"Is your hand okay, Pierre?"

He raised it, appearing distracted, as though he'd forgotten what happened only a few minutes ago. "Oh that. No big deal. Just a minor cut. But I wrapped it, so it won't get in my way while I work today."

It felt like such a relief to see Patti and her Country Kitchen Catering ahead. "Whew, finished my checking rounds. You all ready?"

"You bet I am. What a weekend for Harmony to show off for everyone. Just look at all the restaurants here. Hope the Shady Pine gals can keep up with ticket sales. Looks like it is going to be a hit."

A group of young girls in dance costumes passed by us on their way to the stage. We were happy that the Greensville dance studio director agreed to do a performance. Many of her students came from the Harmony area, so we'd have a built-in audience of family members.

"First act is getting ready, and I have the perfect viewing spot," Patti said. She tipped her head to her neighbor, an ice cream truck. "And with them next door, I'll get lots of foot traffic."

"You've got a wonderful choice of food samples. Look how far you've come with your catering business. But don't you go getting too big to still be our village administrator."

"Don't worry about that, Jackie. I love my job. And I have enlisted helping hands. Charlie is very supportive of my doing this side job. And I have a little one in training to take it over some day."

"Do you think your grandson, Ty, might become part of your catering business? He's not even a year old yet!"

"Can't start them too early. Guy Fieri. Gordon Ramsay. Mario Batali. Tyrone Drake. Sounds like it fits. I have big plans for him."

"Do you think Matt might think Drake and Son and Grandson Construction sounds good?"

"Probably would make more money in construction. But I'll take whatever time I can get with him. Mandy's coming to help me today and she might bring Ty along."

Names are important. I looked toward the Timbers Grill food stand. If it was true what Miguel said about Pierre really being Peter, did it matter? He seemed to run an excellent restaurant, so I say let him have his Pierre name. It was French for Peter, anyway. Close enough.

"But for now, here comes his mom to help," Patti said. "Just in time."

Patti showed me the food samples she had for this event. Small handmade cheese balls in a mini pastry cup with crackers. Caprese salad skewers using early tomatoes. Mini raspberry pies baked in small muffin tins. And strawberry rhubarb bars. She cleverly put her pickled beets, asparagus, and brussel sprouts on small wooden skewers, making them easy to sample.

"Are these the ones Wildwood puts in their Bloody Mary?" I asked, as she handed me one skewer to try.

"Yep, Lynn at the bar there raves about them. And Taliesin's Riverview Terrace Cafe has been using them for over a year. They're big on sourcing their food locally. Now Pierre at Timber Grill is sampling them to use as accents on some of their appetizer plates and charcuterie boards."

"Wow, sounds like your side gig is going gang busters!"

"I think Pierre heard about them from some women who live in The Hills. I've catered several events there. Such lovely homes surrounding the golf course. They did a nice job of using our Harmony Hills to create the course."

I stepped aside as customers were showing up. I was a lucky woman to have the ex-wife of my future husband as a friend. Now that was truly an amicable divorce.

Taking in the activity building around me here on the village green, I also felt thankful for my life in my hometown of Harmony. Aunt Ruth was with her retirement village gang manning the ticket table. My friend Val was across the grounds with her grandson at their hot dog stand. Stu Walters stood by Orin at the Stone Mill's tent.

"Knock knock. Anyone home?" Wanda's hip bump almost knocked me over. She grabbed my arm, laughing and dropping her cheese curds basket as she goofed around. "Darn, I wasn't done with those. Five second rule?"

"Hey you! We're not as agile as we were. No more

surprise from behind attacks." And I was grateful for reuniting with old friends like Wanda, even when she almost took me down.

"Don't be a fuddy-duddy, Jackie. Want to go over to the Brazilian steakhouse with me? I might need propping up when I get near those gauchos serving that meat."

"Sorry, but I'm on duty. You can handle it, Wanda. Maybe Val will take a break and go with you?"

"Looks like they've got quite a bevy of onlookers there already."

"The Real Housewives of The Hills," I said. Wanda's puzzled expression was priceless. "That's what they call themselves. Todd told me about it. He said it was an homage to the Real Housewives television shows."

"I've never seen those, but that group sure looks like they're enjoying themselves. They have years of youthful advantage on me, so I'll bide my time and admire *el gauchos* from afar. Say, are you going to be back later when the band is playing?"

"I sure am. There is a picnic table near the bandstand I have my eye on. Catch up with you here later, Wanda? Now get another order of cheese curds."

Wanda picked up the cheese curds at her feet.

"No, you are not eating them off the ground!"

"Just picking them up to throw out. Think I'll check

out the Wildwood, someone said they had shaved prime rib sliders. Throw a little of their horseradish spread on and I'm in heaven. Ooh, just saw the Asian Fusion restaurant. For sure, I want to check that out."

And off she went.

CHAPTER SIX

Twilight descended over Harmony. I loved this time of day. I'd put my feet up for a few minutes after my long day of walking before I changed into a fresh outfit. The light lavender trousers I'd ordered online fit perfectly, and I chose a silky scarf in the same color. Somewhere I'd read that it looked good with gray hair. I sure hope so.

Todd had brought Libby over to Aunt Ruth, and she'd been hanging at the ticket table all day. I imagined they filled her little tummy with snacks. Soon as I'd brought her home earlier, she had crashed in her doggie bed. We'd both needed the rest before our evening out.

Grabbing a light jacket and Libby's leash, I called for her. "Come on, girl, wake up. It's time to meet our friends and I have a special request from Scott that I bring you along. You two are becoming quite the buddies, aren't you?"

Downstairs Todd had closed for the day, leaving a note with a big exclamation mark saying it had been a good day for the business and that he'd meet me, Celeste, and Felicia later by the bandstand.

"Are you trying to match the sky?" Kim teased as I walked along Main Street.

I hadn't noticed the lavender wash on the horizon. "Well now, maybe I am. Looks like you're ready for a little dancing in that flowing skirt."

Kim did a heel kick and hip wiggle. "I am. My sweet Stu has been taking dancing lessons with me and he has quite the rhythm. Did you see the dance studio classes performing during the day? The adult group opted out of doing a formal stage performance, but there are a few of us who plan to show off what we've learned tonight."

"I had no idea you joined up for dance lessons. Good for you. I'll be cheering you on from my bench."

"Come on, Jackie. You can't fool me. I'll bet you're a terrific dancer. Stu will take you out for a spin. He loves the big band sound, but I don't think MJ & Company play that. I'll ask them though. We can do our swing dance to most any good beat."

"I've never heard of that band before, but I'm looking

forward to it. Someone told me that Ginger is their lead singer."

"She is and can she sing! What a talented gal. And now, like I told you earlier, she's going to be opening a new business here. Did you know she's dating Murph?" Kim loved sharing information, appearing to be knowledgeable. And she was good at it. Her being a successful realtor meant she kept up with what was going on in our community. Her efforts to get some action in the vacant part of the old, closed paper mill were bearing fruit too.

"You're kidding? Well now, I'm doubly excited to hear the band."

"They make the cutest couple. He was with her the first time I opened the old children's clothing store space for her to look at. And the leader of the band is in construction, so he's going to help with cleaning the place up."

"Who is that?"

"MJ Carter."

"You mean Junior? Mitch's son?"

"Yep. Nice kid."

A chill ran down my spine. The mere thought of Mitch Carter brought back memories of that awful time just months ago, when my high school friend Keith Steele was murdered. Mitch didn't do it, but his reputation from the past came up. Kim seemed not to notice, and I was glad because I didn't want to rehash those days. Tonight was a gathering of friends to enjoy food and music. I would not let someone like Mitch ruin that.

"So anyway, Stu's meeting me by the Brazilian Steakhouse to pick out our dinner." Kim licked her lips and murmured, *yummmm.*

"Does that dreamy look in your eyes come from thoughts of the delicious meat you'll soon be enjoying or something else?"

"Jackie! Whatever are you thinking?"

"I understand the gaucho style servers are easy on the eyes. Was that vision dancing in your head? I know you're not that big on red meat."

Kim's tongue peeked out as she winked. "Today, Jackie, I am a lover of red meat. Actually, I may have to go back several times, even if the tasting samples cost Stu four tickets each." She reached into her purse and pulled out her cell phone, almost blinding me with all the glittery crystals on its case. "Oh, he's there waiting now. I must run. I'll look for you at the bandstand."

And she was off.

A shift change was going on at the ticket table. "Anything I can do to help?"

Kay looked up and smiled. "No, I think we're all good. Trudy and I will take it over now. Some vendors are staying open until 9:00, so we'll stop selling tickets shortly before closing. Jeff is coming along to join me at some point."

"Oh good. I'm expecting to find a seat with Aunt Ruth and some of her friends."

Patti was closing her Country Kitchen Catering early and Mandy was helping. At her feet sat an infant car seat. I had to peek in at little Ty.

"He just gets cuter every day," I said.

"Do you want to hold him?" Mandy asked.

"No, that's okay. Let him sleep. Are you staying for the music?"

"Not this grandma," Patti said. "I'm taking Ty home with me so Mandy and Matt can stay and enjoy the evening."

"Please join us at our table. Scott should be here soon too."

"Yeah, I think Matt is coming with his dad, so sure, we'd love to sit with you."

I passed Dermot, who was also shutting down Murphy's stand for the day. "Jackie, nice to see you. Are you still working?"

"No sir. I'm here to enjoy the music and taste more of the food. How did it go for you and Grace?"

"We had a wonderful day, but I'm packing up now and ready to enjoy a brew with him." He pointed to a broad-shouldered man crossing the street and walking toward us.

He looked familiar. Then it hit me. "Chief Murphy? Is that really you?"

He cocked his head to one side and stroked his salt and pepper mustache, not recognizing me. Then it came to him. "Jackie Parker? Joanna and Bob's daughter? You have certainly grown-up, lass. My oh my, it has been a long time."

"How wonderful to see you! I know you retired years ago. Where are you living now?"

"The missus and I moved to Florida. Living the good life there."

"That sounds like a wonderful retirement. Hope you'll join us at our table when you're done here."

"I plan on it. Going to meet my namesake nephew's new girlfriend. She's the lead singer in the band tonight," Paddy said.

"I didn't know they named Murph after you."

"There are innumerable men named Patrick Murphy in the world, but aye, that one you all call Murph was named after me. I understand there have been a few murders since I left and that you are becomin' a well-known local sleuth."

I ducked my head. "There have been a few, but I'm not really that much of a sleuth."

"It should be interestin' to talk shop with my successor Jeff. Will he be here tonight?"

"His girlfriend Kay just told me he would."

I haven't seen Harmony's former Chief of Police since I moved away. My visits here must never have overlapped with his. Our little gathering is growing. Ahead of me on a picnic table, Celeste and Felicia waited with Todd. I saw Val, Chris, and Wanda walking toward me. I was waving at them when suddenly I was grabbed from behind and a hand covered my eyes.

CHAPTER SEVEN

"Scott! You scared me!"

Scott spun me around and gave me a hug. Then, gently brushing back a wisp of my hair, he said, "I couldn't resist. Are you ready to head home, just the two of us?"

"What? No!"

"Just kidding. I'm looking forward to grabbing something to eat. It's been a long day. Come on, looks like our table is filling up."

"Where's Sophia?"

"She's back at Patti's booth. Couldn't resist peeking at her grandnephew. He's quite a handsome young man, if I do say so myself. Which food do you suggest?"

"There's so much. Can't beat Sally's deep fried cheese curds for nibbling, but I'd suggest the Brazilian Steakhouse for more of a meal. The panang curry at the Asian restaurant was amazing. And then there are our favorite pretzel bites with cheese dip at Stone Mill. But the street tacos at Timber River are great too."

"Okay, okay. I get the idea. You've been tasting all day while you were working and loved it all. Now it's my turn. Can I get you something more?"

"Not any more food right now, but I'll try the special beer that Orin brewed just for the festival. Can you carry that all?"

"I'll make it work even if it takes several trips." He leaned down to kiss me. "You're worth it."

"Hey what's that big smile for?" Wanda asked as she and Val joined me. "Wait, let me guess. A handsome man with a hunky masculine physique and the best voice this side of the Mississippi just pulled you into his arms and gave you a big smooch."

"Close, Wanda, but the kiss was a little one," I said. "Come on, Celeste and Felicia are already at our table."

"And so is that jag Mitch," Val said as a sour look crossed her face. "He thinks he's all that, like he did when we were in high school."

Wanda paused, and with a shiver, pulled her hooded sweater tighter against her. And it wasn't from the cold. Her loathing of Mitch hadn't left her, even when it turned out he wasn't involved in the murder of our friend Keith. What happened between Wanda and Mitch all those years ago? I hated to see such a normally happy and content person carry such an obvious weight from the past.

We kept walking toward the table. Mitch was apparently turning on his charms for Celeste and Felicia. Or trying to. They stood near him, and he had them laughing. I glanced at Wanda and saw she was trying to ignore the situation. She walked directly towards the table where Aunt Ruth and her friends sat.

"Hey there, Jackie, how's it going?" Mitch said. "You never told me about your gorgeous friends from Chi-town."

I cringed, but Celeste reached to touch Mitch's arm. "You silly boy. We Chicagoans don't say Chi-town. You must come to our city, and we'll show you the ropes, won't we, Felicia?"

Mitch gave me a wink. "Now that's the best offer I've had in a while." He took a long draw from the beer he held. "Can I buy you two a drink from the limited offerings here? Or we could go to my boat in the marina, where I have some of the high shelf booze."

And here was where, thankfully, Val stepped in. I was painfully aware that Wanda could still hear what was being said, and I hoped to move Mitch along quickly.

"Forget it, Mitch. I just got off hot dog stand duty

and want to catch up with Jackie's friends myself. So bye-bye, big guy." Val had the best expressions and her pinched smile and flick of her hand carried as much weight as what she said.

Mitch stiffened, but quickly regained his composure. "No worries, Val. Your friend sitting there at the octogenarian table might want me to stay. I remember when she begged me to stay."

His voice rose in volume. The final words from him sent Wanda over the edge. She stood, glared at Mitch, and walked directly up to him.

"You are the nastiest, most vulgar, ugliest man I've ever known. I wouldn't want you to do a single thing for me." She turned to smile at the rest of us watching, including us in the torrent of words coming next.

"You think you're such a big guy? You aren't now and you never were. Anything you may consider great about yourself came because of your father. You are nothing. And I hope you get drunk here and…and…" She took a deep, audible swallow before trying to continue, "…and…"

I prayed for Wanda to get herself back together and tell him just what she wanted to happen, but I knew she was losing her focus.

Rolling his eyes and choking back a laugh, Mitch said, "Wanda, you never could stand up for yourself or anyone else." His eyes burrowed into hers. "And you are pathetic."

With that, he did a dramatic bow toward the speechless Celeste and Felicia and strode away, almost tripping over an empty lawn chair, which he immediately launched a kick at.

He passed Scott, returning with our beers, and I was afraid he was going to knock them out of Scott's hands. I quickly handed mine to Wanda. "You need this more than me."

"What's all this about?" Scott asked, looking at our faces.

Felicia laughed. "Dull story. Man hits on woman. Woman shuts him down." She reached out her palm for Wanda to accept a high five. "This classy lady poked the bear without even one cuss word. I had an entire string of them on the end of my tongue, but I held them back."

"Here's to you," Scott raised his plastic beer glass. "I too had an awkward encounter with the opposite sex."

"I hope it didn't end as badly as Mitch's," I said.

"No, certainly not like that. But I barely escaped. It was close."

"And who, pray tell, did you escape from?" Val asked.

"The resort ladies. They were at that Brazilian place oohing and aahing over those guys slicing the meat off the roasts on the long sticks. They tried getting me to buy the caipirinha and have a toast with them. But I stood firm in my resolve to return to my love with her requested beer."

"Which she offered to a needy friend." Wanda seemed to calm down, and I was glad for her. I hoped Mitch would stay away from our table.

"Now I must gird my loins to return to the lioness pit and claim my four-ticket hunk of red meat."

"How do you do it? What a man. You'd better return unscathed and untouched." I grinned up at Scott. "Because you may disagree, but I don't know if you can handle those lady lions. They might just eat you alive."

CHAPTER EIGHT

While all my attention had focused on Scott, our group had grown. Grace and Dermot Murphy, along with his brother Paddy, had joined us.

"That was quite a show," Paddy said. "I thought I recognized the man in the middle of it. Dan Carter's son, Mitch? Kept my eyes on him over my years on the police force here, and he's still making trouble, I see."

The Shady Pines group had pulled yet another picnic table into our grouping. Aunt Ruth, Dorothy, Betty, and Eunice were there, as were Harry and Elmer. The usuals. But tonight, three other elderly men and a couple of other women I didn't recognize were with them. Rocco sat next to Ruth. Nice to see them out together. Sweet relationship at their age.

The band, MJ & Company, was set up on the gazebo stage. The Taste of Harmony committee had done an amazing job of stringing patio style lights around the gazebo and throughout the area so there would be a canopy of lights as twilight descended.

On the stage, I noticed Murph talking with Ginger. Wow, her stage image was so different from what I knew about her as a librarian. She usually dressed modestly and only added lip gloss for her day job. Tonight, with her outfit of a glittery top and skintight jeans, along with an abundance of makeup, she'd transformed into a performer with an eye-catching presence.

Matt and Mandy walked up. "Have you heard this MJ & Company band before? We saw them perform at a friend's wedding last month. They're great!"

Betty agreed. "We had them for our Christmas dance at the retirement center this past year. They can perform music across the decades. Holiday music, country music, folk music, and even a few big band tunes."

"You're so right, Betty," Mandy said. "They really span the decades with their music."

"But what does the MJ stand for?" Betty asked.

"It's for the leader of the group. Mitchell Carter Jr., but he likes to go by MJ. Probably to avoid association with his father," Murph said as he came walking up.

"And is it true you're dating that beautiful lead singer?" I teased.

Murph's big grin told me all I needed to know.

"Wise man you are. I just learned she'll be operating a small business of her own soon."

"That's right, Jackie. She signs the final sales papers on Monday and then the remodeling begins. Ginger is super excited. And if you all have ideas for a name for her new bookstore, offers are being accepted."

"New bookstore?" Aunt Ruth said. "I didn't hear about that. Something Harmony could really use."

"Plus, if it works like we're hoping, Murphy's Coffee will expand," Grace said. "We want to take out the wall, or at least create a big opening in it, in order to bring the two enterprises together. Our customers will stroll over and browse the bookstore, and vice versa."

"Oh, so she's going to take over the vacant spot in your building. Perfect location," Dorothy said. "I agree with Ruth that this will be a terrific addition to our downtown area."

Ava and her friends came by our tables. "So, this is who that gorgeous hunk of a guy belongs to. Well done, Jackie," Ava said with a thumbs up.

"Mandy, we wanted to stop by and thank you for displaying our photographs in your front window,"

Kayla said. "I texted a photograph to my kids to show them their mother is becoming famous."

"My pleasure," Mandy said. "I'm looking forward to running more classes. You guys are the best students."

"Olivia's helping me find the right spot in our home for the one I framed. She has ten times the design sense I do," Phoebe said.

"That forced perspective photograph you took was impressive," Mandy said. "I can understand why you want to hang it."

"Junene, I heard you laid down on a street to shoot yours," I said.

Junene laughed. "I did, but I had my husband and his friend stopping traffic. The cops got a kick out of it."

"Are you staying for the band?" I asked.

"Probably not," Phoebe said. "We had a full day already. Plus, our hubbies golfed and grabbed dinner at the Timbers. We're meeting them for a drink there now. All except Ava, whose husband had a full Saturday schedule fixing up faces and decided not to drive over tonight. All those Botox treatments make for a nice life, though. Hey, did anyone hear how Pierre was doing? The guys working at the Timbers Grill booth said he wasn't feeling well and left early."

"He might have just preferred being at his restaurant instead of here," Olivia said. "Since we're going to the Timbers to meet the guys, we could check in on him."

"I'll bet that hunky Miguel got Pierre's dander up. He has that whole Latin vibe going, but Pierre trying to be French, heh…" Phoebe reached out her fingertip and pulled it back with a sizzle sound. "Miguel is hot."

Murmurs of agreement rose among the housewives. Ava's encouragement that they leave before someone embarrassed themselves was a wise decision by the looks of it. This group could sure attract attention, maybe a television show was in their future.

"And that takes quite a bit for us to be embarrassed," Junene said. "I think we had your man a little shook with our horsing around though. Am I right?"

Scott blushed. Everyone saw it. "I'm just an innocent country boy lost amongst all these sophisticated women. Gosh, I don't know what to do with all you pretty ladies."

"That sexy voice just melts me every time." Phoebe's swoon brought a laugh from Scott.

"Yeah right," Junene said. "I think your fiancé feels you can handle things just fine. Say Jackie, are we still on for that golf lesson Monday morning?"

"Golf? You didn't tell me that," Scott said.

"Oh no, did I give something away?" Junene grimaced. "Sorry."

"It's alright," I assured her. "You've been bugging me to golf this summer and I haven't been on a course for years. I'm rusty and needed a refresher course."

"See you Monday then." Junene and her friends left the village green just as the band began playing.

A small wooden dance floor had been laid down for the evening. Since the dancing hadn't begun, young children were running and sliding across it. An older couple stood arm in arm, watching the musicians get ready to begin.

When the band played a slow romantic tune, couples stepped out and swayed together. But it was Ginger's mesmerizing rendition of Whitney Houston's *I Will Always Love You,* that brought the house down.

At the band's first break, Ginger came to our table and Murph moved over on the bench to make room for her. Everyone was eager to tell her how wonderful she sounded.

"Thank you! I'm so happy to see you all here tonight. It means the world to me. And please feel free to make requests."

MJ stopped by too. "How about you, Scott? Do you have a song you'd like to request? The songs you guys grew up with are some of my favorites, and we've added a few new ones to our playlist at our last rehearsal."

"Thanks, I'll have to think about that," Scott said.

"I'm going over to say hi to my mom and her friends. If you think of any song requests, I'll be right over there."

MJ pointed toward the picnic table where his mom sat. I noticed Mitch was standing a short distance away from his wife. He was looking a little unsteady on his feet as he sipped beer from a plastic cup.

"Looks like your friend has continued his drinking," Celeste said to Wanda.

"He's no friend of mine."

Mitch must have known we were talking about him. He stared in our direction. Then, to my dismay, he walked back toward us.

"Looks like our timid, drab librarian is letting her hair down." He winked at Murph. "Now is the time to take advantage of her when she's all hot and bothered. Dancing up there, rocking her hips at all the men here."

Murph swung his leg over the bench and stood nose to nose with Mitch. "I think you'd better apologize to my girlfriend for those rude comments."

"Ooh, big man. You're not wearing your police uniform now. I'd say that levels the playing field."

"Apologize now, or you'll see what a big man I am, even without my uniform."

One man at Aunt Ruth's table stood up as well, but Elmer pulled him back down. I felt Scott tense up.

MJ saw what was happening too and came running over. "Dad, stop! Leave them alone. Come on back and sit by Mom."

"That witch? Forget it. I'm done with her. And she ain't getting what she wants. Go on up there and play that corny music. See if it pays the bills, cause your mother is planning on draining me dry."

Mitch stomped away, back towards the Stone Mill booth, but not before crumpling and then tossing his empty plastic cup toward his wife's table. I lost sight of him in the crowd.

Wanda watched him leave, a surprisingly calm expression on her face. I was glad to see that. I hated when he angered her. He wasn't worth it. Whatever happened between them in the past had risen to the surface during the time of Keith's death. She never told me what happened, but it sounded like Keith knew about it too.

"I'm so sorry for my father's behavior. Especially whatever inappropriate comments he made to you, Ginger," MJ said. "He can be such a jerk. As you may have surmised, my mother is filing divorce papers. Apparently, Dad is feeling threatened financially. It'll be a long summer. Come on Ginger, time to entertain."

"Well now, that was a mite interestin," Paddy said. "I remember his old man, Dan Carter. He may have been a tough bugger and protected his kid too much, but if he was still alive, he would have given him a kick in the butt for the way he's behaving now. Got his kid out of trouble with power and money, didn't he?"

"And now his wife is going after any money left," Scott said.

Wanda stood, saying she was going to head home. She made her goodbyes to everyone and left.

"Are you okay?" I whispered against her as she hugged me goodbye.

"I am. Just tired. Lots of guests at the hotel mean extra work." She patted my shoulder and left.

I leaned into Scott when I heard the opening chords of the Dolly Parton and Kenny Rogers duet, Islands in the Stream. "Wanna dance?"

Surprisingly, he agreed and hand in hand we went to the dance floor together. I felt the entire crowd being swept up in the beauty of Ginger and MJ's voices.

"That gal can sure sing," I heard Grace say as we got back to the table. "I never imagined it. Reminds me of Sandy who used to sing the national anthem at the football games. And she went to our church. Beautiful heavenly hymns."

"Wasn't that your daughter?" Aunt Ruth said to the frail-looking man sitting across from her.

He nodded and beamed with pride.

Val said, "That's right. Sandy Schuster. I remember her. She's about our age, isn't she?"

The man paled. "She was your age. She's been gone for over ten years now. Car accident in Colorado. But I still have some recordings of her singing and listen to them now and then."

"I'm sorry to hear that," Val said. "It's nice you have those to listen to. And just look at Faye with her friends. She's beaming with pride at her son's musical abilities. Too bad her husband is such a bum."

CHAPTER NINE

I took Libby out for an early Sunday morning walk before the Taste opened up today. We crossed the village green and headed toward the marina. It was so early that our scheduled cleanup crew hadn't arrived yet. Most citizens of Harmony disposed of their trash, and we had no cleanup problems on our streets and roadsides. But invariably an event this size meant the morning light revealed bits of paper napkins, straws, and pieces of food containers. I had to keep tugging at Libby's leash, so she wouldn't end up eating the unidentifiable food chunks on the ground.

Since the Wisconsin River widened here to form Lake Harmony, our marina held a variety of boats. From fishing boats to ski boats. Pontoons to small cabin cruisers. Row boats to sail boats.

The Harris boys were in their hot dog stand to catch any fishermen leaving at dawn who might want a coffee. I stopped in to say hi and chat for a minute. They were pleased with sales yesterday, confirming Val's predictions. Libby snagged a small treat, and we were on our way.

To my right was the marina. To the left the Mary-Go-Round trail edged the village green and continued on toward the Stone Mill Brewery. "Which way do you want to go, girl? We've got a good hour before I have to be back."

Libby tugged me toward the left. I knew what she was thinking. "We can't go all the way to Shady Pines to get a treat for you. Besides, all your buddies there might not be awake yet. I'm leaning toward the marina." But she insisted, and I gave in to her. We'd only walked about ten yards when I saw what she'd sensed.

It wasn't a dog treat she'd pointed to, but a person lying on his back, partially covered by the fringe of ornamental wild grasses that edged the pathway. I bent and pushed the soft plumes of grass aside to see if the person was sleeping off a bender or was injured.

It was neither. A meat skewer stood upright out of his chest. I backed away, letting the grasses wave back, hiding the awful sight of Mitch Carter lying dead at the edge of the Mary-Go-Round trail.

Looking both ways along the walking path, I couldn't see anyone. Pulling out my cell, I dialed Jeff's number. He said he'd be right over.

Large boulders edged the path on the river side of it. I used one to rest on while I waited for Jeff to arrive. From the direction of the marina, Paddy Murphy appeared. He saw me and waved. Then, instead of turning on to the path that would have taken him back to the village green and Main Street, he walked toward me.

"Morning Jackie, you're up early. My brother and sister-in-law get up at one ungodly early hour to get the pastries baked. I've been getting up when they leave the house. I must admit I'm learning to love this quiet time of day. Would you like to join me for a coffee?"

As he bent to rub Libby's head, he caught sight of Mitch's legs. He walked slowly toward the body. His police training kicked in and he was careful not to disturb the grasses anymore than I'd already done.

"I've called Jeff," I said. "He should be here soon."

"Good. Guess we can take a stab at the cause of death." Paddy stepped back away from the body. "I didn't mean that the way it sounded. But with the skewer stuck in his chest, one can only assume."

Paddy's gaze drifted up toward the large food tent just up from us and asked, "The Brazilian Steakhouse?"

I nodded.

"And these are the sort of things they use for their meat?"

"Yes."

Libby started barking when she saw Jeff approaching. I released her to run to him, which she happily did. He squatted, rubbing her back and tummy. "So again, with Libby finding a crime scene. We're going to have to put her on the payroll."

Jeff almost tripped over Libby as he walked toward Paddy and I. "Chief Murphy, you got here before me. What does it look like?"

"Murder by skewering."

"Say that again," Jeff said in a puzzled tone. "Or better yet, I'll look for myself."

I grabbed Libby's collar, so she didn't follow Jeff toward the body.

"Whoa, I see what you mean, Chief."

"Just call me Paddy. You're the chief now. And looks like you have a murder on your hands."

Jeff pulled out his phone and relayed basic directions to the staff at the station. And then, holding his hand over the phone, he asked me if Dr. Potter was still out of town. With my affirmative nod, he ordered that the medical examiner from Greensville be called in.

"Someone will come and secure the area shortly," Jeff

said. "Jackie, if you could stay here until then and protect any walkers from seeing the body, I'd appreciate it. What time does the Taste open today? We should try to keep this incident quiet as long as possible and not have curiosity seekers trampling around here."

"I'll call Patti and let her know about this," I said.

While I was doing that, Murph arrived in uniform to run a crime scene tape across the path. Apparently, Jeff hadn't told him who died because he gagged when he recognized the body at the side of the trail. It was the man he'd threatened last night.

CHAPTER TEN

When Murph composed himself, he set about completing his task of securing the area. Jeff asked me to take crime scene photographs, as he knew I had experience in that area. Paddy offered a couple of brilliant suggestions for angles to shoot and perspectives to use.

It had shaken Patti when I called to tell her about the situation on the trail behind the Brazilian Steakhouse tent. She shared several thoughts about how to keep things on the quiet, asking if they would remove the body prior to the Taste opening. Jeff agreed and said they would be here shortly to take the body in for an autopsy. Patti was glad to hear that and knew the story couldn't remain completely quiet, but she'd let each vendor know about it and ask for respect for the Carter family by not making it a big thing.

When the paramedics arrived, Jeff directed them to park their vehicle in the marina parking lot instead of carrying the body across the village green to the street. Uncertain about removing the skewer, the paramedics asked Jeff if they should transport the body with the skewer in place. The image of a tentlike structure being transported on a gurney would look awkward. Since deputies had already taken fingerprints from the skewer, Jeff requested it remain in the body, thinking it might facilitate the medical examiner's job. While his staff processed the scene, Jeff left for Mitch's home to let Faye Carter know about her husband's death.

Paddy joined Libby and me as we left. "Sorry you had to see all that. I imagine you're glad to be done with the seedier side of life."

"That I am."

"You come from a beautiful country. I've photographed in Ireland several times."

"That it tis," he said. "Do you have a favorite area there?"

"I especially loved the western side of the country. The dramatic Cliffs of Moher. Beautiful Kilkenny Castle. Stunning Ring of Kerry. Am I getting carried away? Maybe I can convince Scott to travel there with me one day."

"She's my homeland and I try to get back to see family there every so often. I don't think the whole of Ireland has the crime my brother Dermot says you have here in Harmony. He says it's been on the uptick since you arrived."

I shrugged. "I've gotten questioned about that and I'm at a loss why."

Paddy let out a belly laugh and said, "Just teasing you. Harmony is a delightful little town. From my cousin Seamus I hear that Los Angeles, with all its natural beauty, has some mean streets."

"I have a half-sister and niece who live there. What area does your cousin live in?"

"He never lived there. He's still back in Ireland. It's his daughter Katie who lives in LA. The lure of California with its beaches and glamor called her."

"So, you have family on the west coast too?"

"Yes ma'am. She's a strong one, but I think her parents sense that she's burning out. Best I can read from my cousin, he is trying to convince her to leave the hustle and bustle and danger of the big city behind. At least take a break for a spell."

"Maybe she'll come visit you in Florida. She'd still have a beach."

"True, but not the glamor! I'll suggest it to Seamus and let him pass it on, so she doesn't think we're ganging up on her."

"The old Irish pushing the young?"

"Exactly. Plus, the missus and I are opening an Irish style pub. Did you know pub stands for public house? I have such fond memories of the pubs back in Ireland. They were our neighborhood gathering spot. Anyway, we bought an old two-story building and are rehabbing it. Can you believe it? Two old fools she calls us. She might be right, but I need something to do. Only so many crosswords and jigsaw puzzles a person can stand. If Katie shows up, her youth might give us ideas on what to do with the place."

"Your town is filled with only retirees?" I asked.

"That it's not. Since it's an affordable area, there are lots of vacation rentals and second homes for those from the inland areas. Folk like to get out to the Gulf during the hot, humid summer weather."

"I wish you much luck with it. My fiancé's sister and her husband live in Tallahassee. I'll have to see if she knows about your town. What's the name of it?"

"Seaside Cove, a charming little town. We feel very lucky to live there. Have a good day, Jackie, and perhaps I'll see you again before I leave. But not another meeting like today."

. . .

he Taste opened at eleven o'clock. The church crowd, who might otherwise go to Dolly's for breakfast, or the Wildwood for brunch, found their way to our village green, many of them lured by the polka band due to play soon.

I'd made the rounds to let the vendors know there had been a disturbance on the river path, but it was being straightened out and the show would go on. Jeff, deciding not to draw attention to his presence, remained dressed casually, as though he was here at the event just to mingle and enjoy the day like all the other guests.

We talked after he'd returned from meeting with Faye Carter and he told me that MJ and his mother insisted on coming to the crime scene. "That gave me a good chance to ask Faye a few more questions, like what she thought when Mitch didn't come home last night. She told me it wasn't unusual. That when he'd been drinking, he sometimes went to his boat to sleep it off, and not always alone. I thought that sounded plausible and it gave me the idea to search his boat. Was Mitch going to meet someone? A person who might have meant him harm?"

"Or maybe the spouse of that person who might be waiting for him on the boat?" I added.

"True. Anyway, MJ asked me to keep him in the investigation loop as his mother just couldn't handle something like this now. She's taken a sedative and will be knocked out for the rest of the day. He told me he loved his father, but that their relationship was complex. His response to my asking about knowing of anyone who held a grudge against his father was that sure, he could name a few."

"I think we all could. Mitch Carter was a lightning rod for trouble."

"He also mentioned that he's noticed Mitch wasn't as strong as he once was. And that his grandfather, Big Dan Carter, died from heart issues. He left saying he'd send me some names. The kid looked pretty broken up."

"Have you been to the marina? It's close to where I found him. Could be someone saw something out of the ordinary."

"I haven't yet. But I will check out his boat, so I might ask around if anyone saw something. When he left your group last night, did you notice which way he went?"

"He headed toward the Stone Mill booth."

Jeff looked in the direction I'd indicated. "That would be next to Miguel's. I went to interview Miguel, but other than giving me a quick confirmation that the skewer came from their tent area, he's been busy."

"Might be avoiding you. It must be unnerving to come to a small town and end up having a man murdered with your restaurant's skewer stuck in him and lying behind your tent. Could the killer be here today?" I asked.

"Sure, he could. By the depth that skewer was in, I believe it was a man who did it. Would have taken some strength. At least we've lifted some fingerprints from it."

"It seemed like a small amount of blood from such a deep and nasty wound."

"It might not have bled much initially. Knife and sharp instrument wounds can often be like that. They sort of seal the entry wound. That's why I wanted the coroner to see the exact angle the thing went in."

"And to have me photograph it. But why were you and Paddy both so specific about angles to shoot the skewer at?"

"It makes a big difference. It could be critical in whether the murderer is right-handed or left-handed, short or tall. Was Mitch advancing or backing away when he was stabbed? It gives us a more concrete perspective."

Jeff and I continued walking around the grounds. We went slowly by Miguel's Brazilian Steakhouse to see if he was free to talk. Miguel saw us and jerked his head, motioning us toward the back side of his tent. Away from prying eyes.

"We know the trouble Mitch gave you and your crew yesterday," Jeff said.

"Yes. The man thinks he is an American cowboy. Is that how you say it? But our gauchos are good men. We do not stab a drunk, slobbering and running his mouth off. My skewers are valuable and carefully locked together every night. Something must have been missed last night. For that, I am sorry. How someone got one I cannot tell you. But none of us would do a thing such as what happened to that man."

Kim and Stu stopped us as we came back out into the main area. "Still no Pierre. One of the workers told us he was getting worse last night!" Kim seemed especially anxious about Pierre not being here.

"That's too bad. What is the matter with him?" I asked.

"Some of his symptoms, according to a guy here, points to food poisoning! His staff is running this place and the restaurant. What if either place is putting out contaminated food? We can't let this go on. The Taste will be shut down."

"Kim, dear, don't get all crazy talking like that," Stu said. "We don't know anything for sure just yet."

"Oh, good grief. Let's find out. We should check on him right away. If someone here is serving poisoned food, it could be awful."

"Keep your voice down, Kim," Jeff said. "I'll check if anyone else has gotten sick. When did he first have symptoms?"

"He went home early on Saturday," I answered. "It could be stomach flu."

"In June? We have to nip this in the bud, Jackie. Kay must know about this!"

"I know that the county health inspector had been here Friday and Saturday observing how the food was being handled. He'd been very pleased with it. He even did some random instant testing, and everything seemed normal. So, calm down Kim. Unless someone else gets ill, nothing more needs to be done. Stu, look, the polka band is going to be starting."

He caught my cue. "She's right. Come on, sweetie. Let's kick up our heels." Stu took his wife's arm and steered her away.

CHAPTER ELEVEN

The Shady Pines group was off duty today because Kay and a couple of committee members offered to take over the ticket sales. But they were in attendance and when the polka band started cranking out dance tunes, they were the first ones on the floor. Soon, a familiar and lively song got more couples up and stepping in time across the dance floor. Several of them comprised two women, which was not uncommon here in Wisconsin. Men either bowed out or were in short supply at many dances. Unlike modern dances or country line dances, the polka was best done with a partner. Dorothy's granddaughter grabbed Eunice to dance while Dorothy and Harry took a turn on the floor. Aunt Ruth and Rocco added an extra half step and flicks into their style while Kim and Stu struggled. Apparently, their dance lessons didn't extend to the polka.

As I prowled the Taste watching for underage drinkers, I also talked with vendors to find out how things were going for them. We'd be sending them a survey after the event to see where we could improve and what worked particularly well, but I wanted to be available now if they had questions about Mitch Carter.

Much to my surprise, the only one who asked me about it was Orin. He promised to keep it quiet. He knew Mitch well from all the times he'd been at the Stone Mill and was sorry to hear of his death. I gave him no further details but told him I appreciated his discretion. We needed to finish up the event today and let Jeff work on figuring out what happened last night.

It appeared to be another blockbuster day for ticket sales. Luckily Sally was prepared with rain checks to hand out to customers when she ran out of curds. Smart businesswoman! Good way to get new clients to see her entire product line at the Collins Cheese Shop.

I wanted to make sure that the restaurants that weren't local were happy and would take part if we held this event again. The Asian restaurant agreed they certainly would. They attracted many locals but also tourists who'd never heard of them. The Mexican food truck people were delighted as they made contacts for future business at parties and picnics.

As I walked by the Timbers tent, I asked if anyone heard how Pierre was doing now. One server took time to tell me he'd gotten a call from Pierre late last night to see how the day went. "He sounded pretty tired and kind of out of it, but said he'd be okay with another day of rest. He was sorry he wasn't here to help us more. If he wasn't doing better soon, he would go to a Critical Care Center. But when I called this morning with some questions about closing up later, he didn't answer and hasn't returned my call yet. Maybe his phone died, or he's sleeping."

"*W*ill someone check in on him at his condo later?" I asked.

He pointed toward Miguel's booth. "A couple of his female friends over there said they would be glad to check in on him."

Perfect, the housewives were at Miguel's and that was my next stop. Ava and Junene stood by while Phoebe was busy booking her husband's birthday party into a private party room at the Madison restaurant.

Miguel welcomed me with a smile as I walked up.

"Ah, my lovely photographer friend. You have had a very successful event, no?"

"Thank you for saying so. By the looks of it we have."

"We were just talking about giving Miguel more business," Junene said. "Especially since he voluntarily checked all his meats after our friend Pierre had an upset tummy and remembered eating some of the meat here."

"I am so disappointed. You didn't say who was ill. You only said your friend." Miguel made a gesture as though he were spitting. "I'm sorry the man is ill, but he has it out for me. I know he is a fraud. Pierre…hah his real name is Peter. Probably using a fake name because he has left angry restaurant owners in the past that he's trying to avoid now. He knows I know. Coward. Fraud."

Whoa, I thought. Miguel's reaction seemed over the top. The housewives were as stunned as I was.

Miguel pulled himself together. "Please excuse my reaction. What happened has unnerved me. I must go back to work. I look forward to making your husband's birthday an event to remember," he said to Phoebe.

Ava had stepped aside to take a call. With an anxious expression, she rejoined our group and told us that Pierre has gone to the clinic, and they'd admitted him to the Greensville hospital.

"Oh no," the rest of us said in unison.

"He's being taken care of. They are dealing with dehydration now but were questioning me about what food he came in contact with."

"Why are they calling you?" I asked.

"I guess he put me on an emergency contact form. That's all I can think of. He probably doesn't have anyone else local to help with that. He told the hospital staff he ate meat from Miguel's and food from Patti's. It sounded like they're thinking it might be a case of botulism poisoning."

Ava's expression changed. She seemed confused.

Junene put an arm around her. "It'll be okay. Like you said, he was dehydrated. Once they get liquids in him, he'll be on the mend. He probably put you on the hospital form because you're a nurse."

Ava looked up at her. "You could be right. That would explain it."

I hadn't heard about Pierre sampling Patti's offerings from Country Kitchen Catering here at the festival. But then I guess I hadn't asked. Why would I? His not feeling well was turning into a potential case of food poisoning. Good grief. So maybe Kim was right after all.

CHAPTER TWELVE

One more thing to worry about. Hopefully, it was something else, and once Pierre got hydrated, he'd be okay. I knew we'd had good luck keeping people from knowing about a murder happening during the night, and I was hopeful we'd keep any hint of tainted food from spreading. I noticed a committee member was quietly slipping around with the instant test strips the health inspector left. Somehow, they'd gotten wind of it. Could the hospital have notified them? But things were wrapping up here, so we'd made it through.

I walked over to say hello to Aunt Ruth, but before I had a chance, she grabbed my arm. "What on earth happened? I just heard there was another murder in Harmony. Did you hear about it?"

With a sheepish grin, I said, "I did."

Ruth placed her hand over her heart. "Please don't tell me you found the body. I don't know how much more our family's reputation can take."

"Hey, I can't help it if I'm just on a walk with my dog on a beautiful Sunday morning and a body is blocking the path."

"True. One must approach life practically at times." Ruth pursed her lips. "But please, Jackie, spare me the details this time. Every time you get involved with these things, I end up answering all the questions our villagers have. And it's wearying."

"You poor dear. I'll refrain from mentioning anything further about it." I zipped my lips shut and turned to walk away.

"Oh, but one question!" Ruth called after me.

I kept walking, working hard not to giggle.

"Jackie, honey."

I kept walking away.

Soon I felt a tug at my elbow.

"Is it true he had a meat skewer stuck in his chest? Should we be afraid that there is a stranger in our midst? Someone who came to our safe little village for the Taste and brought danger and death with them?"

"I thought learning details were oh so exhausting for you. Dear Aunt Ruth, I want you to be healthy and happy. I would never want to burden you with the nitty gritty of a horrific murder scene." I grinned mischievously.

Rocco was nearby and saved me. "Ruth, you shouldn't bother our local detective. But Jacqueline, I hope you won't have to be chasing down the murderer. You and all the workers here deserve a week off after this hugely successful event. Please let me know if there is anything you or Jeff need help with."

"I'm hands off on this one," I said.

"So far," Elmer cautioned. "We've heard that before."

"He's right, you know," Eunice said. "You are proving to be both an attractor of nefarious crimes and a sleuth at solving them. Come on Ruth, let's head back to Shady Pines. The guys are going to Shorty's to play cribbage. Kay said she doesn't need our help to pick things up. But she's looking for you, Jackie."

"Okay, thanks Eunice." I gave Aunt Ruth a quick peck on her cheek. "Thanks for all you guys did to make this festival happen."

Kay was talking with the members of the polka band as they packed up their gear. "Jackie, I was wondering if you've heard any more about how the chef from the Timbers is doing. I sure hope no one else here gets ill. Not the kind of publicity we need. On another note, did you see the Madison paper featured our festival?"

"I just heard from Ava, one of the Real Housewives of the Hills…"

Kay burst out laughing. "Don't say that too loud. I think some of them are still here."

"No worries. They started calling themselves that. They can be a fun bunch. I've gotten to know some of them through Mandy and her classes. But anyway, Ava just spoke with the hospital."

"Hospital? He's that sick?"

"He went to a clinic, and they admitted him. Might be only dehydration, but they wanted to find out what he's eaten recently too."

"I suppose it could be some other food borne issue, but I've not received any news of others getting ill. It could be something else entirely. Thanks for all your help, Jackie. Oh, and for keeping the news about Mitch quiet. Poor guy. His family must be in shock. Since I didn't grow up here, I don't know all the family issues, but I've been hearing the Carters had quite some reputation. Still, nothing to deserve what happened to him."

"Agreed, Kay. I'll help wrap things up here."

"Thanks Jackie. Appreciate it."

. . .

Scott and his sister Sophia were sitting on the bench in front of my studio, waiting for me as I walked over from the village green. I was a lucky woman to have found such a wonderful man at this point in my life. And he came with a built-in family. Yep, all in all, things are looking good for you, Jackie Parker.

"Sorry I made you wait," I said, unlocking the front door to the studio. "Sophia, I've got that print you wanted framed and ready. Want to take it with you tonight?"

Sophia stepped back to look at the photograph of the river view from Scott's balcony. "This is perfect. Thank you. I'll have to tell Mandy I appreciate her input on the mat and frame. It'll be such a treat to hang up in my Florida home. I'll always picture sitting on Scott's deck and taking in this view. When are you two coming down to visit me?"

I looked up at Scott. "We were considering coming to visit in January."

"Good time to get out of the snow and cold here," Sophia said.

Scott nodded toward me. It was the signal that we were ready to share our surprise with his sister. "It would be for our honeymoon."

"Oh, my gosh." Sophia ran to hug me and then Scott. "You are one smart man, big brother. I'm thrilled for both of you!"

CHAPTER THIRTEEN

*R*elaxing last night was enjoyable. I wished Sophia and her husband lived closer. It would be nice to have a sister nearby. But then my thoughts turned to gratitude that at least I'd be gaining one! No grumbling about distance, Jackie. And remember, you have one in California too, which means traveling ahead for Mr. and Mrs. Scott Drake.

But right now, I needed to get going for my golf lesson with Junene. I hoped to improve my game, which was a low threshold, as I'd only played a handful of games in my life. Now, with a more relaxed lifestyle, I looked forward to becoming relatively competent at golf. Images of us playing on the Driftless Course here in Wisconsin, in warm Florida with palm trees, and overlooking the beach in California spurred me on.

I parked my car on the street last night, so I left using the studio's front door. Through the windows of the Cut-N-Curl, I saw Val opening her salon for the day. "Hey girlfriend, I see you survived the weekend too."

"Thanks. How did you do with your grandsons at the hot dog stand? I saw them early yesterday morning, and they seemed pleased with how it went."

Val snapped open a pink protective client cape, dropped it on one of her pink swivel chairs, let out a big dramatic sigh, and plopped down in the chair. "Look at me. I'm in my sixties and just spent over twelve hours on my feet smiling and putting hot dogs in buns. Now another day on my feet. Getting too old for this."

"Are you still trying to find someone to buy your business?"

"A competent hard-working partner with half a brain would do, but it's the patience, skill level, and drive that they need. A few graduates of the beauty school in Greensville have approached me, but they don't show promise. They wouldn't fit with my clientele either. Pink hair, shaved off on one side, is not a styling request I get around here."

"Maybe it's the future, Val. Keep an open mind, as you told me."

"Oh, I am, believe me. I'm openly deciding they won't work here." She pushed herself up and checked her calendar. "For instance, today's clients are Constance with her weekly set and comb, Eunice is getting her quarterly perm, Wanda has her scheduled root touchup, and Phyllis will get her short, practical cut again. Does that sound like an interesting workspace for missy pink hair? The business end of things I could handle for years, though dreams of selling the entire thing, lock, stock and barrel, dance through my head." Val plopped back down in her beauty chair. "But that's for another day."

"Catch you later. Say hi to Wanda. It surprised me she didn't come down on Sunday."

"Me too. Enjoy your golf lesson."

As I unlocked my car door, I noticed Paddy and Jeff were having coffee together inside Dolly's Diner. Stay out of it Jackie, the voice in my head told me. Maybe Aunt Ruth was right about my involvement with murder cases. How did that always seem to happen? My curiosity is usually the cause. But then the last time I got involved, it was because the victim was an old high school friend. And how could I not have helped when Eleanor Harmony needed to discover what really happened to her fiancé? But this time, other than finding the body, I couldn't see a reason to even walk inside and ask how the investigation was going. Except I was a sort of witness to the argument between Mitch and Faye. Well, not really. I was at a distance from them.

Go to your golf lesson, Jackie, and stop thinking about it.

My watch told me I'd be early. I jumped when a voice said, "Go in. You know you want to." Val leaned out of her shop door, giving me a shooing gesture, before letting the door close behind her. She must have seen me hesitating on the sidewalk.

From inside the diner, Dolly held up the coffeepot she was carrying. I nodded. Another coffee. Just for a moment, I told myself as I stepped inside.

"Good morning. You two putting your heads together?"

"Just catching up on Harmony happenings," Jeff said. "Where are you off to this early?"

"Golf lesson. Can you believe it? Scott wants me to go out on the Driftless Course tomorrow and my skills are sorely lacking. Thought you were hitting the road early, Paddy."

"Well, let's just say my plans have changed. Shorty got me hooked up with his cribbage group. Pretty wild and crazy guys. This was supposed to be the day I left bright and early to get home, but last night at Shorty's also turned into a bon voyage party, which meant we drank a few toasts. I decided I'd wait until Tuesday morning to leave. I'm driving and I love road trips but I'm also liking being back in Harmony."

Dolly came by with my coffee. "Cribbage? Glad to hear my guys are back. Elmer and Harry keep to Shady Pines most days, and Sta rarely comes in to see his brother. Paddy moved away. What's a girl to do?"

"We love you too, Dolly." Paddy said. "How'd old Claude do for you at the Taste?"

"He nailed it. Course, without Vivian, it would have been different. I made an appearance, but they didn't even need me. They loved all the yakking they got to do with everyone. And they came back with all sorts of interesting gossip. Can't believe that about Mitch being stabbed. What is this town coming to? Bet you have lots of suspects. The guy had plenty of enemies."

"God love her, she never changes," Paddy said as Dolly walked away. "But we were just talking about the case. Jeff here said you've been helpful in some cases, and he was hoping to ask you a couple of questions about this one."

Jeff squirmed uneasily.

I let him dangle out there for a few seconds, remembering when he'd dismissed my ideas before. "That's nice of you to say I've been of help, Jeff. Thank you. I appreciate that."

"I just figured you knew Mitch from high school."

"High school was a long, long time ago." I stopped there. Sure, I was curious, but I didn't want to tip over into being nosy. If he wanted my opinion, he'd have to ask directly for it."

"Sounds like old Dan Carter's kid had a few issues." Paddy took a sip of his coffee and peered over the rim, keeping his eyes focused on Jeff. When Jeff didn't speak, Paddy set his cup down. "What were you just saying about his son looking through the business's books and records to see if there is anyone who's been sending threatening notes or having an unusual disagreement with him? Did you notice anything odd Saturday night, Jackie?"

The question came from Paddy, not Jeff, but it was what I thought about telling him. "He stopped by our picnic table Saturday night. He'd been drinking and was confrontational. The distasteful remarks he made to Ginger were inappropriate and Murph let him know it."

"My deputy? He threatened Mitch?"

"My nephew? Glad to hear he stood up to Mitch," Paddy countered.

"Whichever way you choose to take it," I said.

"I'll ask Murph about it," Jeff said. "He didn't tell me that happened. MJ told me about his parents heading to divorce."

"Mitch had some unkind words to say about that," I said.

"But like I told you, Jackie, and I think Paddy will agree, it took some strength to stab the skewer in that deep. Especially because he would have seen it coming. I couldn't tell if there had been a scuffle. I have some prints to work with and now alibis to check out."

"Don't forget that Latin lover guy," Dolly added as she poured us more coffee. "The one with the spinning meat stuff. Vivian told me all about him and Mitch having a heated argument."

"Oh, really?"

"Really," Dolly answered. "Probably all the testosterone they have flying around inside them. Men!"

CHAPTER FOURTEEN

ulling into the parking lot for the Driftless Golf Course clubhouse, I noticed the course was busy. This must be the men's league. Well, good for the Driftless. They not only brought seasonal tourists in to help our economy, but they were a welcome place for locals as well. How long ago was it that I visited the condo models sales office? That memory brought up more murders I'd been involved in. Yikes! Maybe I could see why my connection to murder cases was being brought up more and more.

Looking out across the rolling hills, I made out the roofline of the old Harmony mansion, now a museum and nature center. What a pleasing view. Groundskeepers kept the course in tiptop shape and well groomed. They randomly scattered numerous flowerbeds as though nature had created them on her own.

Junene said she'd meet me here at the clubhouse. We'd just be using the driving range and putting green for practice today.

I heard my name called out and turned to see Orin waving at me from the seat of his golf cart. "Morning Jackie, I didn't know you golfed."

"I don't, really. But I'm going to have a refresher lesson and try to get into it this summer. We'll see how it goes."

"I'm looking forward to getting out on the course after the long weekend. But it was well worth it. I enjoyed meeting your former police chief, Paddy Murphy. He is very interested in the brewing we do. Sounds like a nice place he's opening in Florida."

Stu came walking up with Junene. "Look who I found! Tells me she's a golf pro and going to work with our own Jackie Parker."

Junene pinched Stu's rosy cheeks. "You are just the cutest. Enjoy your play today and remember only one mulligan. Maybe you'll all enter the golf tournament we're going to be having."

Stu, with even rosier cheeks now, grinned. "You bet we will. See you later, Jackie. Have fun!"

"What's this about a golf tournament?" I asked.

"You all might not appreciate this course in your backyard but believe me, the golf world does. The rentals in the lodge and houses on the grounds are being snapped up for the summer. With the Chicago and Milwaukee markets alone, it would be successful, but they are coming in from lots of other states and even a few international golf fanatics."

"The world? Goodness."

"Well, to be honest, I only know about my cousin from England who's coming to visit me," Junene said with a grin. "She's a golfer and we're going to play. But seriously, at least from across the United States."

"You are a good ambassador. When is the golf tournament?"

"In September. We're running it as a benefit for the Harmony Museum. I'm working on my contacts for prize donations and the businesses in town that are willing to be involved as well. We're even getting a couple of Wisconsin golf stars to play."

"I hope you find some way that Parker Studio can contribute."

"Oh, have no doubt. I will make lots of suggestions."

Junene had an awesome swing. I was in expert hands. We were about halfway through our bucket of balls when I thought to ask her if she'd heard how Pierre was doing.

"I don't know. But the girls were going up to the hospital to check on him this morning. I expect to hear something when they get back. Let's practice some putting. The short game is where rounds are won or lost."

"What's the big attraction for Pierre?"

"It started with us meeting up at the Timbers bar for a drink. He'd invite us to stay after they closed, just to hang out and have some laughs. Most often during the week when we might be here without family or guests. He's younger than us, but hey, we were having fun. We enjoyed his company, and he liked us. He's really a very witty guy."

"I first met him when we photographed the food he'd be serving at the Taste. He seemed very nice. You all must have become close friends. Ava was very upset when she heard he'd been hospitalized."

"Ah yes. You noticed that. I did too. Ava is a registered nurse and with a business degree to boot. She met her husband when she went to work with him in his dermatology practice. After they married, they both agreed it was better they did not work together. So, she's a wifey now with access to free Botox! Gotta love how that worked out. She comes up here by herself pretty often. Gets a little restless. No children. Bored. I think she enjoyed those evenings more than the rest of us."

"Are you saying what I think you're saying?"

Junene was setting up a putting drill for me. When all five balls were lined up, she stood. "Did they have an affair? Probably. With cell phones, you don't have to be at home to answer your husband's good night calls. And here he can't watch the home security cameras like they have back in the suburbs. Know what I mean?"

Now I watched as she stuck tees in on either side of the five balls. "These tees show if your starting swing is on the intended pathway."

I took my time doing the drill and sank three of the five. "Like this?"

"Good. Your putter face was square to the ball. That's it. You're a natural."

I blew on my knuckles and rubbed my chest with them. "I didn't tell you I have a few miniature golf championships in my past."

"You were holding out on me!"

After we'd finished on the putting green, Junene brought the subject of Pierre up again. "But back to Ava and Pierre. There seemed to be some tension between them lately. I think Friday night they had a falling out. Out of what, I'm not sure. It could all be in my imagination."

"Maybe he just wasn't feeling well then already. Did

you and your husbands all hang out with him at the Timbers that night?"

"That was the plan. Until Ava unexpectedly joined us. Alone. Her husband was supposed to be in, but I guess he was delayed. Heaven help us. Maybe Pierre is pretending to be ill just to stay out of sight from the flock he's attracting because confidentially, I think Phoebe was making her moves too."

"You're kidding."

"Just a sense I got. Could be totally off base," Junene said.

"This is feeling like Peyton Place. But you're too young to remember that show."

Junene let out a knowing laugh. "That must have been a cutting-edge show in those days. But if you ask me, I think Pierre's been pushing her away. He has a business here, and messing around like we think they were couldn't be good for his job."

"And for her marriage," I said. "Maybe he found someone outside of the Hills world and she got wind of it?"

CHAPTER FIFTEEN

The gift shop in the main lodge featured my own photographs for sale, so I decided to stop in there and see if their stock was up to date. Murph, in his police uniform, was inside the lobby.

"Good morning, Murph. It was so nice to share the evening on Saturday and hear Ginger sing. She has an impressive voice."

Murph grinned from ear to ear. "Thank you. I agree. Sorry about all that happened when Mitch picked on her, but gosh when you found his body Sunday morning…who would have imagined?"

"I talked to Jeff this morning about if you have any more leads on what happened."

Murph clenched his jaw. "To be honest, Mitch went through life leaving enemies in his wake. Most people learned to blow him off. But he could sure build up rage in a person. I know by my reaction Saturday."

"Since you're in uniform, I guess you're not playing in the golf league." My curiosity meter was flashing. Why would he be in the lobby? Had there been a break-in at one of the condos?

"I wish I was, but I'm here to talk with the restaurant staff."

"I understood they admitted Pierre to the hospital with dehydration."

"That's correct. A friend took him into the clinic yesterday because his condition was worsening. They sent him to the hospital," Murph said. "Now the hospital has notified the county health department and contacted us. They've confirmed he's experiencing botulism poisoning."

"But I thought that was deadly," I said, thinking this news was not good on so many levels.

"I looked it up myself. I mean, we were all at the Taste, if that's where it came from. Apparently, it isn't as deadly as we all think," Murph said. "And there were no other reports of illness over the weekend. The staff here did a thorough disinfecting of the restaurant kitchen, even though everything tested negative."

"So why are you here, Murph?"

"It seems the source might be something in his own kitchen."

Like maybe a jar of Country Kitchen Catering's pickled vegetables? I kept that thought to myself. "Did you find anything suspicious?"

"He wouldn't grant us access. He nixed that right off the bat. Pierre said he knows there's nothing in his condo that he could have gotten it from, and he'd prefer no one go there without him being with them. He expects to be out of the hospital soon and if they haven't pinned down the source, he'll have his food checked. It's not a danger to anyone else, were his words."

I left The Hills Resort with concerning thoughts about where Pierre might have gotten the infection. Where did the toxin hide and grow? He waited a long time to get himself checked out. Was he afraid it might have come from his own booth at the festival, and he didn't want to sound an alarm? That would have been a very selfish move on his part. More people could have gotten infected. Or did he think it occurred in the Timbers restaurant? Again, that wouldn't have spoken well of his character. Or it might simply have been that he really wasn't that ill. It couldn't have been a deadly dose, as his first symptoms appeared days ago. Things progressed, and now he was hospitalized for dehydration and diagnosed with a botulism infection. What other places could he have gotten it from?

Again, Patti's cute labels on brown kraft paper for a simple country feeling kept popping into my head. He had wanted to test samples of her products. What if they discovered a jar belonging to her on the kitchen counter of Pierre's condo?

But right now, I needed to hustle home to change. Scott had made plans for Sophia, Celeste, and Felicia to join us on *Playin' My Toon*, Scott's pontoon boat docked in the Harmony Marina. The three of them were leaving for Chicago today. Celeste and Felicia would drop Sophia off at O'Hare to catch her flight back to Tallahassee.

Todd was going to be there too as he'd been one of our Chicago group before deciding to move to Harmony for a few years. His work at Parker Photography was invaluable. He handled not only usual issues with the studio, but more importantly, had created an online store and was a whiz at social media promotion. I hoped he'd stay right here.

Things were quiet at the studio. Aunt Ruth was there today, as usual. She covered the shop on Mondays because she enjoys seeing how things are going. It helps me too of course, as she knows the family business inside and out. On top of that, she's been like a mother to me, and I enjoy seeing her.

"Getting back into the game so you're ready to take on golf with Scott tomorrow?" she asked.

"I hope he's patient with me. I've heard that couples golfing together can get ugly pretty quick."

"I imagine you two will be fine. You're probably a better golfer than you think, and Scott strikes me as a patient man. He looked like he was ready to pounce on Mitch on Saturday, though. Glad MJ got his father to leave. And now he's gone. Sudden deaths are always hard to absorb, even when they happen to an unpleasant person. Still, I feel bad for MJ and Faye. He was their family."

"Did you know they were divorcing?"

"I didn't. Sorry to hear that. Does that make Faye a suspect in her husband's murder?"

"I suppose she could be. So often it is the spouse. But don't ask me. I'm trying to stay out of it."

"But you found the body, Jackie. You are part of it whether or not you want to be."

"Finding a body and investigating a murder are two quite different things, Ruth. Guess who arrived at the crime scene right after me? Paddy Murphy, Dermot's brother."

"I like Jeff very much, but gosh, I miss Paddy. Those were the good old days. And I miss them some days more than others."

"Even though you're working in the very spot you worked for all those good old days?" I teased Ruth. "And now you have your favorite niece living in Harmony with you? That hurt my feelings. I'm crushed."

"Don't talk such nonsense. You know I love having you here, but just wait until you're my age and there will be things you remember fondly too. And things you are happy to let fade away," she said in a wistful tone.

"I'm sure you're right about that. I will try not to let regrets linger long, but happy memories remain forever."

"Now off with you, my dear niece. Your pontoon awaits and I, forward-looking woman that I am, am going to explore that new POS system you had installed. My brain could use some exercising."

"Good for you, my computer savvy auntie!"

"A lifelong learner, as I like to call it."

"But now to change into more seaworthy attire and collect my Libby for our outing."

Ruth's head bent down toward the computer screen,

her reading glasses resting on her nose. I was a lucky niece. Aunt Ruth had seen me through and shielded me from my parent's marital problems and had always been a refuge after they passed on.

CHAPTER SIXTEEN

The clang of sailboat riggings greeted me as I approached the harbor. The river widened enough to entice sailboat owners to harbor here too. They picked up summer winds and sailed across Lake Harmony even as the Wisconsin River flowed beneath them. The campground on the other side of the lake had been seeing families come to the Driftless area for a long time. And now The Hills Resort brought even more tourists to our special part of Wisconsin.

Tony, Val's oldest grandson, was working at the Harbor Dogs food stand. A couple of kids his age waited in line to order. I had to admire how hard working both Thad and his older brother Tony were. Chris and Val had instilled a good work ethic in their son, Travis. He ran the municipal marina, owned the Harbor Dog, and recently had taken over the local boat storage shed and named it Harris & Sons Marine Maintenance.

I waved at Tony, but he didn't see me. Instead, it appeared the teenage girls walking along the path distracted him. I chuckled to myself. I understood why his eyes would follow them instead of me.

Next to the marina office, a new store and bait shop had recently opened. Construction was underway for storage of seasonal rentals of water sport equipment like kayaks and paddle boards. Travis's boat storage area kept pontoons ready for tourists to rent. With more visitors using it, the harbor area was taking on a new look. I know Patti and the village council were deeply involved with trying to keep the small town feeling while making sure dock space was available for both locals and out-of-towners.

Scott was buying bait in the marina store while his pontoon was being gassed up at the marina fueling station. I saw Rocco on board his boat, the *RoccoMe Baby,* doing some of the never-ending tasks boat owners have.

"Request to come aboard," I called up to him.

"Come on aboard, Jacqueline," Rocco answered. "What a delightful surprise! What brings you here?"

"We're taking my Chicago friends and Scott's sister out on the pontoon for a little enjoyment of our June weather. They're all leaving later today, so it seemed the perfect way to spend their last hours here. And I saw Scott getting bait, so maybe some fishing is in store for us."

"I didn't know you enjoyed fishing," Rocco said. "And I will admit I didn't picture it being something your friends were interested in doing, either."

"Never judge a book by its cover," I scolded. "Celeste and Felicia both fish for salmon and lake trout in Lake Michigan. Celeste's brother owns a fleet of offshore fishing boats with guides for groups to rent."

"The deep sea feel, only on an inland lake. I stand corrected. I do sometimes miss Lake Michigan for boating."

"Do you regret moving your boat here? And now you even have your own house here too."

"I try not to dwell on regrets. Doesn't mean I don't miss things about Chicago and the lake, but can't be everywhere. Still, like yourself, Jacqueline, I keep a small place in the city when I want to slip away. Maybe Ruth will venture with me there one day. We could take a Lake Michigan tour boat and enjoy the beautiful Chicago skyline from the water."

"You're a wise man, Rocco Montalvo. Aunt Ruth and I were just talking about not letting regrets linger. I'm glad for the special friendship you and she are enjoying."

"Thank you. I am as well. Did you know Sophia and her husband keep a boat in the Florida town where Paddy lives? Small world."

"I didn't know that. You certainly are a source of knowledge. Maybe they'll visit Paddy when he gets his dream Irish style pub opened up," I said.

"It's nice when a couple can have a getaway like that. You and I are retired, so it's easier for us. Suppose it's the equivalent of what they call Up North here in Wisconsin."

"True. I've heard of families having summer cottages only a couple of hours away for a relaxing escape."

"Sounds like it."

"Speaking of boats, which one is Mitch's? Can I see it from here?"

Rocco pointed out the pier with Mitch's boat dock. "Have you heard any more about what happened to the man? I suppose his son will keep the boat and continue to use it. Mitch Junior seems like a nice young man."

"I've heard bits and pieces." I didn't enjoy being so evasive, but I didn't want to be spreading unproven tidbits of information bordering on gossip. "Did you ever notice Mitch entertaining on the boat?"

"Yes, I did. He had many outings with his buddies. Fishing, drinking, that sort of thing. Rarely did I see his wife or his son onboard. Why do you ask?"

"Faye, his wife, told Jeff that he'd sometimes spend nights on his boat. Sleeping off a night of drinking…or for other unnamed reasons."

"I don't like gossip. But if this helps in the Chief's investigation, I will say that yes, he would. And if I may be so bold, not always alone. Might the fact that I noticed someone near his boat Saturday night be of importance?"

"It could. I found him on the path between the village green and the river. The marina is not far away. Can you tell me what you saw?"

"I'd driven Ruth home to Shady Pines and decided to check that everything was secure on the boat. With so many strangers here because of the Taste of Harmony, I was concerned. I'd notice them wandering around here in the marina and looking at the boats. I talked to Jeff this morning when I saw him boarding Mitch's boat, but would you like to hear it also?"

Here I was asking questions about a case again. I had to extradite myself from this habit. But maybe just a little listen to what Rocco saw Saturday night. What would that hurt?

· · ·

*O*ur lazy afternoon on the lake was perfect after the busy weekend I'd had. A wonderful distraction from Pierre's poisoning and Mitch's murder. Double trouble for Jeff. It was relaxing to watch Scott entertain my friends and help them find good fishing spots. He was so sweet. And Libby loved standing on the seat and letting the lake breezes blow against her. Her sea legs had vastly improved over the many times she'd been out on the water.

Sophia talked about her meeting up with Paddy in Seaside Cove. "Isn't that cool? He lives where we have our beach home and boat. I offered to give him some tips on party and event planning and how it can totally change the dynamic of a business. I'm excited for him and eager to see the place. We've made plans to visit when Jack and I head down there in July. Inland Florida gets hot and muggy then."

"That's so nice of you to share your knowledge with him. I hope Scott and I get down to see you all soon. But first there's another thing I'd like to talk to you about."

"Sure, what is it?"

"Hold on, I want to get everyone's attention. Scott, could you pour the champagne please?"

"Celeste and Felicia, we have been friends for many

years and I'm so grateful for your visit here to Harmony. It means so much to me to maintain our friendship."

"Even though you left us behind in the big city for this precious but very little, restaurant-starved village?" Felicia asked.

"Yes, even though that happened."

"And you stole Todd away too?" Celeste pointed out.

Todd laughed. "Hey mine is only a temporary change of scenery."

"How do you define temporary, Todd?" Celeste asked.

And Felicia chimed in. "Please don't be toasting to your selling your loft in River North."

"No, I'm keeping the loft. But now, back to this toast. Sophia, Scott is blessed to have you as a sister and soon I'll have a sister-in-love. This is leading to an important question for all of you."

Scott poured a plastic champagne flute for each of us, and as I looked at these important people in my life raising their glasses, I said, "Would you be my bridesmaids?"

Todd was the first to speak. "Thanks, but no thanks."

That got everyone laughing, but then I saw confused looks crossing their faces and I took advantage of it.

"I didn't start out planning a full blowout wedding. It was never my dream. I would probably have just gone across into Iowa or eloped to Las Vegas, but then I decided that seeing our friends and family with us sounded good. And I began thinking about the time of year. December. Red crushed velvet bridesmaid dresses would be perfect. It would be so Christmassy, especially with pumps dyed to match. Maybe white glittered feather boas or edging on the dresses. The ideas just kept coming. I love the look of bridesmaids in more of a hat. I'm torn on that one and welcome your input. Would you like a small pillbox style or fur trimmed hoods? For your bouquets, I'm dreaming of little, teeny tiny Christmas presents nestled in evergreen boughs. Not big ones, but enough to have the scent of fresh evergreens in the air as you walk down the aisle in front of me."

The first one to speak was Celeste, who said in a dry tone, "This is a surprise coming from you."

"It hit me out of the blue. I remembered all those wedding photographs taken by my father and Aunt Ruth. I remember looking at the wedding party's photographs we'd put in the window. All I wanted then was to get out of this small town and explore the world. But now I'm back and ready to do one of those big weddings. I want you three to stand up with me. So, what's your answer?"

"But Jackie, you're older than the brides in the

wedding photos taken back then. Isn't that a more youngish thing?" Felicia asked.

I let my head hang and my shoulders drop. Taking a peek up from under my drooping eyelids, I saw they all still held their plastic glasses in the air. Quietly, sadly, I spoke. "I thought you'd like to share in our special day."

After a stunned moment, Celeste said, "Oh, we would, honey, but I don't look good in red."

Felicia was the first to give me the evil eye. "Celeste, I think our friend is pulling our leg."

Scott, who'd been in on my little stunt, kissed me and said, "Before you all have strokes, we are having a small ceremony, but a big celebration and you can wear whatever you want. Libby will be Jackie's maid of honor. She looks good in red."

Then he took a sip of champagne, and everyone joined in the toast.

CHAPTER SEVENTEEN

Scott and I said our goodbyes to Sophia, Celeste, and Felicia with lots of hugs and promises to keep in touch.

"You were outstanding," Scott said. "I could hardly stop myself from laughing as I watched their faces fall in disbelief."

"Thanks for helping me do that." I kissed Scott. "Now off you go to that job site. Hope the issues got cleared up."

Leaving the marina on my way back to the studio, I noticed Jeff sitting on the bench next to where I'd found the body. He appeared deep in thought, and I hesitated to disturb him. But he looked up and called my name. "Hey Jackie. Enjoy the pontoon ride?"

"I did. Beautiful day for it. We caught a few fish and had a few laughs."

"Nice, Jackie. Can I have a couple minutes of your time?"

"I really should get back to the studio."

"Please."

He looked seriously distraught. And I had to admit to myself that I was curious about who might have been on Mitch's boat that night. According to Rocco, it wasn't the first time he had guests. Might be a clue as to what happened.

So, I stayed.

"Jeff, you have an experienced police chief who knows this town to help you. I think he would be a better person to talk with."

Jeff held up the Murphy's coffee cup he was holding. "I did. Spent the last hour with him at the coffee shop."

My insides wished for a cup of Murphy's coffee too. It always helped me think better. I sat down next to Jeff. "Talk away."

"I haven't gotten the autopsy report yet, so that will help direct which way I go," he said, resting his elbows on his knees and staring into his coffee.

"What do you need to know? Isn't it obvious that a meat skewer being shoved into his chest killed him?"

"Paddy put a different perspective on that when he remarked that there wasn't much blood on him."

"You told me that since the skewer wasn't pulled out, it could have sealed the blood inside the body. If the skewer hit a vital organ, he'd have died immediately, right?"

"That's true. But Paddy asked me to consider that Mitch was dead before he was stabbed." Jeff rubbed his temples and leaned back. "That possibility hadn't occurred to me, but it's plausible. If, say, he'd had a heart attack, he wouldn't have bled outside the wound. His heart wouldn't have been pumping blood."

"You're suggesting that some random person shoved a skewer into his dead body? Is that what you're asking me to believe?"

Jeff pinched his lips. "Something like that. Things aren't always what they appear. But it also could have happened that he was arguing with or threatening someone. That he was so worked up he had a heart attack."

"Sure, I get that. But the skewer? How did it get in him? Why was it in someone's hand to begin with?"

"That's where I'm hoping you have some ideas."

"Could Mitch have been threatening the person, so he grabbed something to defend himself? Maybe they'd been arguing, and it was getting heated. Still, to have the skewer in his hands, it must have been more than a quick reaction. I doubt a meat skewer was just waiting there in the grass. If Mitch had the heart attack, fell over, and as a final blow instead of trying to revive him, the person stabbed him with it would mean he had bad intentions all along."

"Paddy also offered a scenario where Mitch lunged toward the person and the man or woman raised the skewer to defend himself. Only Mitch clutches his chest and falls forward, impaling himself on the skewer. Then the person realized what went on and shoved against him, making him land on his back."

"Jeff, you just said it could have been a woman. Why? I thought the force to drive the skewer in would more likely come from a man."

"Not if Mitch's falling body weight caused it to enter his chest," Jeff said.

A wave of nausea washed over me. Wanda's hate had stewed and bubbled beneath the surface for decades. Could it have come to this?

Jeff continued talking, explaining that he'd checked for fingerprints. "I got MJ and Faye's prints and didn't find them on the skewer. Miguel and his workers had alibis. There are one person's prints I haven't gotten to…"

I was listening through my haze until I heard the

name I was dreading to hear. Wanda. No, he didn't say that. It was in my head. He hadn't said her name.

Jeff gave me an odd look but continued. "…gotten to identify. And that unknown set of prints could be our murderer. Of course, they can wipe fingerprints off, so I've been gathering alibis too. His wife said she was at home alone. That she left after being embarrassed by her husband's behavior. His son performed in the band and Ginger said the last time she saw him was when they packed up their gear at the end of the night and he drove off. Miguel was still at his site late as they have a lot to do to close up. Ginger saw Miguel was still there when she and the rest of the band left. He always checked the site after these sorts of events, making sure things were buttoned down tight. Apparently not too tight or we wouldn't have found that skewer. Miguel mentioned seeing a figure walking alone along the path toward the marina as they were finishing up."

"He did? Did he have a good description? It was dark. Was he sure it was a woman?" I asked.

"I didn't say Miguel thought it was a woman," Jeff answered. "Did he say something else to you?"

"No," I mumbled.

"He could see the person was wearing light colored pants and had a hood pulled up like they didn't want to be seen. Jackie, why are you acting so weird? I'm just mentioning it because Rocco saw this same figure in the vicinity of Mitch's boat."

My heart was racing. I had to calm myself. "Rocco told me you searched the boat."

"I have. It appeared someone had been there. Not sure if it was a man or woman. Typical beer and food in the refrigerator. But there were lights left on. Had a woman, an unknown lover maybe, been there waiting for him? But if she's a married woman, it could have been a jealous husband waiting to sabotage him. That would complicate things for me. I need to find the person. She or he might not be involved but could be a witness."

"But they stabbed him before he got to meet the person on the boat."

"That's the way it looks." Jeff shrugged and stood up. "It wasn't like there was a struggle on the boat. It all happened right here."

CHAPTER EIGHTEEN

*J*eff paced the path in front of me. He mumbled something about the power of hate. I knew what kind of hate could grow inside a person, eating away at them. I thought of Wanda and something she had said.

"What is it, Jackie?" Jeff asked.

"Umm…" I couldn't tell him what had crossed my mind. Not yet. It couldn't be true. I needed to talk to her first.

"Jackie, I know you thought of something more. Spill it."

He was right, but I wasn't ready to share all that was swirling in my mind just yet. Instead, I pointed out another fact. "Mitch's circle of enemies is wider than you talked about. There were many people who heard him on Saturday night. People who might have come in for the festival and been reminded of unpleasant encounters with Mitch. The skewers were handy, whether it turns out for offensive or defensive purposes. Maybe you should go further outside of the people you mentioned."

"His son gave me names of workers and suppliers fed up with the way Mitch does business. From missed pay checks to unpaid invoices. MJ's grandfather, Big Dan Carter, may have manipulated people, used his power and influence to get his way, but he paid his bills and his employees. Mitch didn't have the charisma or minimal ethics of his father. I admit I had little interaction with Dan before he passed away, but Paddy mentioned knowing him and the legend he was back in the day."

I was relieved to hear that Jeff was increasing his scope of the investigation. "Personally, I couldn't understand how MJ worked with Mitch. They were so different."

"Playing in a local band might be a fun side gig, but it doesn't support you. Remember the kid started his own roofing company as a way not to work directly with his father. But he still was under his thumb and control. Seems like a nice enough kid. He didn't appear too crushed by his own father's death."

"Maybe he's just trying to appear strong for his mother?"

Jeff shrugged and took a long sip of his coffee. "I'm left with another puzzling situation. Miguel said they accounted for all skewers each day. Did someone else know how to get to the skewers?"

"Can't help you with that one, Jeff. Gotta run."

I dialed Val's cell phone as I walked away.

Val picked up. "Hey! How was the pontoon ride?"

I had Val cracking up about the bridesmaid stunt I pulled on Celeste, Felicia, and Sophia.

"Oh my god, that's hilarious! Now I have the visuals of my wedding popping up. Remember how your white straw, or was it plastic hat wouldn't stay on?"

"I do. And Chris' mustache got trimmed at the wrong angle because he was so nervous."

"The photos will never let him forget that. And Wanda's dress not covering those horrible swimsuit sunburn lines?"

"Speaking of Wanda, did she show up for her hair appointment yesterday?"

"She didn't. And that's not like her. I was worried she might have eaten something that made her sick, like Pierre. I tried calling, and she didn't answer. Then I called the front desk of the Riverview and Nadine told me that Wanda was fine, just busy. Nadine handed the phone to her, and she told me she was sorry but had simply forgotten her appointment. Didn't stay on the line long. Gave me some excuse about a maid not showing up and being busy with guests from the Taste checking out. I let her go."

Val knows Wanda better than I do. They've seen each other often over the many years I lived away. "She seemed so upset Saturday night. Do you think that whole Mitch thing from years ago came back to her mind?"

"I know it crossed mine," Val said. "She got strange when all that stuff with Keith was going on. Edgy. Distracted. Remember when we tried asking her more directly about what happened? She said Mitch was capable of evil."

"I do. Then she told us she was all grown up and able to put the incident in perspective. But she never told us what specifically happened."

"And I suppose when she heard about Mitch's murder, she didn't feel like coming back to the Taste on Sunday. Don't blame her."

I was passing the Harmony Happenings offices and noticed Stu was still in. "Gotta go, Val. If you hear from her, please call me."

"Will do."

Stu looked up from his computer screen with one of his big smiles. "Welcome, Jackie."

"Surprised to see you still here."

"Putting the final touches on the paper for Tuesday. Sending it off to the printer shortly. What's up?"

"I don't mean to bother you, but remember how you helped me solve Keith Steele's murder by researching old news articles?"

"I do. We discovered the Williston connection. It was fun. Scratched the investigative reporter itch I still get occasionally. What can I help you with?"

"They do not report juvenile offenses in the paper's police blotter. Is that right?"

"Depends what time period you're thinking of. Back in the day, the kid's name would not be published, but the incident might have been. The perpetrator would have just been listed as a juvenile."

I explained to Stu what I was looking for and he said, "I'll get on it in the morning."

CHAPTER NINETEEN

Tuesday morning started with me nervously switching outfits for my first golf game with Scott. The white boatneck pullover with my khaki capris looked classy. But isn't there something about having to wear a collared shirt at golf courses? Or is that just for men? A classic Ralph Lauren polo shirt in a heavenly shade of blue would work with my white cuffed shorts. I'd be wearing a collar just to be safe.

Libby gave me her approving head tilt. "If today goes well, Libby, I think I'll treat myself to a shopping spree at the pro shop of the Driftless Course."

We had an early tee time. Since Scott had to leave for work right after the round, I agreed it was better to meet at the course. And selfishly, that would give me a chance to shop on my own. Within minutes of arriving, we were on the tee box of the first hole.

"So glad they let us go as a twosome instead of pairing up to make a foursome," I said. "I'm nervous enough without having a stranger waiting for me to swing."

"Relax, Jackie. I'm no Tiger Woods myself," Scott joked. He stopped his warmup swings to watch me tee off.

One down. A decent hit off the tee. Good drive. Ball in the air and it stayed on the green!

"Nice form, Jackie. I'm impressed."

"Now I hope it's not one and done."

Scott's drive went twice as far as mine. But I almost caught up with him with my next hit. I reached for the score card placed in a holder in our golf cart, but Scott stopped me. "No scoring this go round. That can wait."

"You're sure? I can take a loss." There was a competitive side of me, but secretly I was grateful because I didn't need the pressure of scoring.

My third shot got me near the green.

"You're not a novice golfer, Jackie. That was an excellent shot."

"I've golfed before, just has been a very long time. But thank you, I'm thinking this will be a great way for us to get out into the fresh air besides taking walks and boating."

"You certainly make use of that Mary-Go-Round trail. After we're married, you can use the trail right behind our place to get to it."

"About that…"

"Whoa, you're not planning on me living in your apartment above the studio, are you?"

I laughed at the thought. "No. There's barely room for me and Libby up there. But what I was thinking is that when I'm moved out, I want to use the second floor for additional studio and shop space. And I'd like to get into your construction schedule so we could be ready to start with it by the spring of next year."

"Or you could move in with me earlier and have it all done by Christmas," Scott suggested with a wink and a nudge. "Think about that!"

"Nice thought, but I can wait."

We finished our round without me totally embarrassing myself. Then, with a glance at his watch and a quick kiss, he left for his work site. They took my rental clubs out of our golf cart, and I turned to walk back to the pro shop. I noticed Jeff's police cruiser outside the main resort condo building. Two mornings in a row that the police are here. Wonder what it is this time.

The pro shop held a lot of inventory. After the round

today, I was feeling more confident knowing there would be golf in my future. I'd rented clubs today, but buying a set was in my long-term plan. A cute outfit was more immediate and easier to make a choice on.

After trying on several things, I chose two outfits. First choice was a white skort, a short-sleeved turquoise top with white edging, and a coordinating zip front vest. Next, I chose a bright summery green skort with a yellow top. Add two visors and a set of golf shoes to the pile and I was ready to check out.

Jeff's cruiser was still here. Curiosity got the better of me. Had he come across the missing jar of pickled vegetables? The front desk clerk told me that Chief Mathis was upstairs in Pierre's condo.

"Pierre's coming home from the hospital is good news," I said.

"No. I thought you knew. I'm so sorry to tell you, ma'am, but he passed away early this morning."

I was shocked. Dead? "What happened?"

"That's all we've been told so far. Excuse me, I must answer that phone."

Turning slowly, trying to absorb what I'd just heard, I almost ran into Doc Potter.

"Oops, excuse me," he said, touching my arm. "Jackie, are you okay? You look a little pale."

"I just heard some upsetting news. Pierre, the chef

here at the Timbers restaurant, has passed away. You've been gone. Maybe you had heard he was ill for a few days. He went to the hospital yesterday. I heard he was dehydrated. But that doesn't kill you. Does it?"

"It can, but that isn't what killed him."

"Wait, how do you know? You've been gone."

"Jeff called me to meet him here as soon as he learned Pierre had died. He told me a poison was the cause. Would you do me the honor of coming with me to the condo? I'd like to have you with me when Jeff explains what has been going on with Chef Felton."

"So that's his last name. I never knew it. It was always just Chef Pierre. If you don't think Jeff will mind, I will go up to the condo with you."

"I don't believe he will. He speaks highly of your intuitive skills. And I also join him in appreciating your way of looking at things which helped solve some rather complicated murder cases. In fact, when I saw you by the front desk, I thought Jeff had invited you here to help."

"No, I just got off the golf course. Scott and I played our first round together."

Doc looked at the large shopping bag at my feet. "And now it looks as though you're stocking up for future outings. I love golf. Don't get to do it as much as I'd like, though. How did you play?"

"Pretty good, actually."

"But now, shall we?" Doc walked me to the elevator and stepped aside, letting me enter first. He pushed the button for the third floor.

"Jeff's brought you in to get your opinion on how the toxin got into Pierre's system?"

"He did. Botulism is an illness caused by a toxin. The bacteria are called Clostridium botulinum. I spoke with his doctor at the hospital to get a better idea of the progression of symptoms he experienced."

"Probably terrible stomach pains, right?" We moved out into the hallway of the third floor and the elevator door closed behind us.

"There might have been some of that, but the disease usually begins with weakness and feeling tired. He experienced those things on Friday."

"So that's why he left the Timbers early on Friday night. Not to get away from the housewives, but because he was so tired."

"What do you mean? Housewives?" Doc looked at the wall sign, directing us to condos by the number. "This way, Jackie."

"They are a group of women who own houses or condos here and like to hang out at the Timbers. Ava is one of them. Yesterday I heard about him leaving his restaurant early Friday night. So now that makes sense."

Doc nodded thoughtfully. "The symptoms would have progressed over the weekend. He may have experienced continued weakness in his limbs. Maybe vomiting or diarrhea too."

"I can see now why he might have hesitated going to the doctor earlier, thinking this was a summer flu."

"If he had gone in earlier, it doesn't mean they could have saved him, but the odds got worse the longer he stayed here alone," Doc said, stopping in front of Pierre's condo.

The door stood propped open with a drooping potted plant, badly in need of water.

nside Pierre's condo unit, we found not only Jeff, but also the county health inspector who'd been alerted to the botulism death by the hospital. The county considered it critical that they find the source of the poisoning.

"I've already cleared the restaurant he managed and have obtained all the necessary contacts from the food festival your village put on over the weekend. The deceased's abode would seem to be the next best place to search and test." The inspector was all business, explaining the rapid tests that we'd used at the festival could sometimes show false positives, but rarely missed the active microorganisms in this bacterium.

I introduced myself and explained that I was a member of the Taste of Harmony committee. "I can assure you that we are committed to discovering the source of the contamination. Hopefully, it's here so we can put an end to this."

"And the health department has the same goal, Ms. Parker. Food poisoning would be unpleasant words to attach to a food event that saw hundreds of people pass through. This appears to be a slow acting bacterium, so finding the source will be critical in our path to containing it. And until then, all potential sources will be under scrutiny."

Doc asked if any other cases had shown up at clinics or hospitals.

"Not yet," the inspector answered. "But as I said, in Mr. Felton's case, the botulism appears to be slow acting and from the hospital's account, he felt what we think were the first symptoms on Friday."

I interrupted. "Then it can't be the food at the festival."

"You'll note that I said we think. Many things could have caused his first symptom of being tired," Doc said. "And it will react differently in different bodies. The best thing is not to assume and to continue searching. The window is still open for other people to have contracted it through the same food, but not identifying why they don't feel well."

Here Jeff asked a question I'd had as well. "But isn't

botulism like this almost always a fatal thing? Like killing off people in masses?"

"It can be. But it is also all around us in our soil, most commonly in spore form," the inspector said. "The spores are generally harmless, but they can grow and turn into active bacteria. And as in this case, forming a neurotoxin affecting the central nervous system. But enough science, let us begin the search and perhaps lay this mystery to rest."

I wondered how long we could keep this new information under the news radar. Eventually it will make its way to the online Harmony paper. What a mess. But being here will be my chance to find Patti's jar of pickled vegetables and hopefully clear her. The refrigerator was the most obvious place for it, but the inspector was in my way. Maybe the garbage. Would Pierre have thrown a glass jar out after sampling it? Or would he have put it in recycling?

The counters were a mess of dishes, glasses, and silverware. A large chef's knife lay on a chopping board. It looked like he'd been cutting vegetables. A small bowl held chopped onions, now discolored and slimy looking, and another held tomatoes. The board held remnants of red from the tomatoes. An uncut celery stalk lay next to it, along with three additional plum tomatoes. Apparently, he'd been preparing something before he became ill.

I couldn't just go tipping the garbage out, but Doc was already preparing to do that on a large paper spread on the hall floor. His gloved hands began carefully separating nonfood trash from leftover food.

I found Jeff in the bedroom at the back of the condo. "Hi Jeff. Full plate for you this week."

"You've got that right. What are you doing here?"

"I ran into Doc in the lobby, and he asked me to join him. Plus, I have something I needed to let you know. Patti remembered Pierre had taken one of her jars of pickled vegetables to sample for potential use as a relish or adornment for dishes at the Timbers. I'm worried. It would look bad if her prepared food caused Pierre's illness."

"It would look even worse if it caused his death. Why didn't she say something earlier?"

"She submitted everything in her booth to testing, but she forgot he'd taken this from her earlier in the week. He promised to sample it and let her know if he was interested in ordering a batch."

"Go and let Doc know to keep an eye out for it."

Doc apparently had overheard us. "Is this it?" He held up a small jar with Patti's labeling on it.

My knees weakened. The opened jar wasn't completely empty of product.

"Guess he didn't care for it." Doc set aside Patti's small jar and an empty soup can. Balled up paper towels and a tissue box were put in another empty garbage bag. A half empty sleeve of saltines was set to the side with the soup and Patti's jar.

The inspector came in and took the food items.

My eyes roamed. I could tell Pierre holed up here by a blanket and two pillows on the couch. Tissues laid crumpled on the floor and three empty diet soda cans sat on the coffee table in front of it. The drapes were drawn. The air was stale.

Suddenly, Ava appeared at the open door. Her red, swollen eyes broke my heart. They all really cared for him. I went to give her a hug and extend my condolences, at which point a sob escaped her.

"I don't mean to be overdramatic, but this is just so sad. He will truly be missed by us all here in the Hills."

"You must have been very important to him."

She startled. "Why do you say that?"

"To have him list you as a contact at the hospital," I said, surprised at her reaction.

She let out a breath and cleared her throat before speaking. "Oh yeah, that. He was like family. And with no real family close, we all did what we could for him."

"Did you see him over the weekend?" I asked.

"You mean like Saturday? I didn't. But I think Phoebe brought him a few things to settle his stomach. I'll go check the bathroom if you want to see if he had taken any medicine."

"That's okay. Jeff's back in that area. He probably had the same idea as you."

Ava's fingers tapped against her thigh as she began pacing, her eyes darting around the space. "I'll have to find a family contact for him."

Jeff came walking out of the hall saying, "Quite a love nest back there. Oops, sorry. I didn't know you were here."

Ava laughed uncomfortably. "That's okay. We house-wives had an idea that he entertained a few young women up here."

Doc looked up from his task in the hall. "He was a patient of mine and gave me a sense he liked the ladies too." He set aside a bloody bandage with the food items.

"Why are you keeping that?" Ava asked, barely able to control her trembling hands. "It looks gross. Just throw it out."

"I don't know if you're aware of this, but the bacteria can enter the bloodstream through an open wound. It doesn't have to be ingested."

"But I was told you couldn't get it through skin," Jeff said.

"Not on the skin's surface, but through a deep cut," Doc said.

"But how would it have gotten in there? Like maybe it was on food, and he rubbed against it? We still would have to find a source, correct?" Jeff asked. "Maybe he cut himself slicing and dicing and it was on the vegetable?"

Doc just shrugged and kept digging.

"Or…" Jeff held up something he'd brought from the back. "This empty wine bottle might explain the cut and the broken wine glass back there in the bedroom. He had been drinking."

An excited shout came from the kitchen. "Positive! I might have the answer to where the toxin came from. This small jar tested positive."

Oh no. Not that. My worst fear.

The inspector came walking into the living room area where Jeff stood with a wine bottle and Doc was on the floor sorting garbage.

"Do any of you know this…" He took the jar and read the label. "Country Kitchen Catering Enterprise. Were they at the Taste?"

Ava spoke up. "I know her. We've used her for catering parties. I'm shocked. She seemed so on the up and up. Yes, she was at the Taste."

I was quick to jump in. "But my understanding is that Pierre got this from Patti Hunt, that's the owner's name, earlier. Not at the Taste. He was considering using it in his restaurant."

"That would fit with the timeline," the inspector said thoughtfully. "I'll call her and notify her to pull any of this product and verify that none was sold at the Taste. This may be an open and shut case if it turns out to be the source of the botulism and not a false positive. But I'll continue to do immediate tests on the rest of the items you've separated out as well."

CHAPTER TWENTY-ONE

In the lobby I saw a sign taped to the doors of the restaurant that read *Closed until further notice.* But the door was open, and a few staff were meeting at a table near the kitchen.

I hated to interrupt their meeting, but I wanted to let them know it appeared the source of the botulism that killed their boss was found, much to my personal dismay. It will crush Patti when it turns out that her pickled vegetables tested positive.

The inspector found toxins in a jar in Pierre's condo, I told the employees. I started to leave but made a split-second decision. "I'd like to ask you a question. On Saturday morning, I saw Pierre with a bandaged hand. Do any of you know what the injury was and how it happened?"

Of the five people gathered, four shook their heads no. One spoke up. "I remember seeing that bandage Saturday morning too. I don't know how he got it, but the last time we saw him on Friday he said he didn't feel great, so if we could manage without him, he'd go upstairs and rest up for the big event on Saturday."

"That's right," another one said. "I don't know how it happened or when, but it was a noticeable and substantial bandaging job. Chef brushed off our concern and said he'd be fine. That a cute nurse had made sure it was okay. I figured he went into an immediate care clinic and had it taken care of. Why are you asking about it?"

Without getting into an explanation of what I'd seen upstairs, I said, "I was just wondering if he ended up with the wound getting infected. But since he went to a clinic, I suppose they handled it appropriately."

On my way to the village offices to give Patti the bad news, I made a phone call to the Stevens Dermatology offices. Without giving my name, I asked to speak to Dr. Stevens. I mentioned I lived in Harmony and knew his wife. I led him to believe I was interested in Botox treatments. He said he'd be happy to set up an appointment if I'd like. I brought up the Taste of Harmony and he offered me the information that he was sorry to have missed it but that he had late hours on Friday night and some Saturday appointments, so he didn't get over to their home in Wisconsin this past weekend.

"And what was your name again? Perhaps we can talk about treatments the next time I'm in Harmony."

I created a dead zone, fake cutoff voice and disconnected the call.

The news about Patti's food testing positive had to be delivered in person. I relayed the inspector's instructions to have her pull any other containers of it in an abundance of caution.

"I feel horrible. How could that have happened? What did I do wrong?" Patti was obviously distraught. This was her worst nightmare.

"We all know you did nothing wrong. You're very careful in your kitchen. The health inspector asked you to call him. Here's his card. These things happen. Pierre should have gone in sooner, instead of letting himself grow dehydrated and weak. The housewives were helping him but couldn't drag him to the hospital. But Patti, when did you last see Pierre before Saturday?"

"Let me think. Probably was Friday morning. He was

making sure that the Timbers booth was getting set up properly for the start of Taste on Saturday."

"And you were in the offices here or out on the green Friday?"

"In and out. The village offices are quiet on Fridays, so I wanted to be available if the committee had questions. Like about power sources, stuff like that."

"Did Pierre have a serious injury on his hand when you saw him?"

"Not that I remember. Why do you ask?"

"Odd thing happened at his condo when we were there searching for a source of the botulism."

"Why are you asking about an injury?"

"It seemed someone was with him Friday night at the condo. There were things that showed he might have been entertaining. I'm wondering if his guest brought food and didn't leave any containers behind. I'm trying to find another probable source of botulism. Plus, it looks like he was injured there. Maybe cut himself while chopping vegetables. We found a cutting board, knife, a bloody bandage, and a broken wineglass in his bedroom. Did he say anything to you about plans for Friday evening?"

"No, I just assumed he'd be working at the Timbers, as usual."

"I've learned that he handed the evening duties off to

his staff, saying it had been a long day setting up and he was going to retire and rest up for tomorrow. When I saw him on Saturday, he had the bandage on his hand. It was wrapped such that someone would have had to help him with it. Professionally administered. So, if I knew what happened, I might find out who was with him. The staff thought he went to a clinic to have the cut treated. I'll ask Jeff to check on that."

"Are you suggesting someone brought him other food and that might be the source of his poisoning?" The hope rising in Patti's face was hard to watch. "But hadn't he opened my jar and tasted the food?"

"The jar was opened, and some was gone. But I don't know that he ate it."

"Where did you find it?"

"In the garbage."

"You know how to hurt a gal. Thanks for letting me know he didn't even like it."

I knew she was kidding to hide her hurt. "Sorry about that, my friend."

"But I don't understand, Jackie. If there was botulism in my food, doesn't that mean it's where he got it from? Are you grasping at straws here? I don't do well with false hopes."

"Speaking of false, the inspector said the test strips sometimes showed false positives."

CHAPTER TWENTY-TWO

Give me a good movie on the big screen, and a bag of buttered and salted movie theater popcorn and I'm a happy person. Our double date with Kay and Jeff to the senior discount movie night was just what I needed. Walking out to our car after the movie, I asked if anyone wanted to stop for a drink somewhere.

"Thanks, but I've got a long day ahead of me tomorrow," Jeff said. "I'd better skip it. You three go ahead."

Kay gave his arm a squeeze. "Not without you. Let's catch dinner together on the weekend. Maybe we could make a night of it at Miguel's Brazilian Steakhouse in Madison?"

"Give me a couple of weeks before asking me to

watch big skewers being carried around and my dinner sliced off of them," Jeff said.

Scott made an offer they couldn't refuse. "I haven't done a cookout for you all on my deck recently. How about we plan that for Saturday?"

"That sounds great," Jeff said. "What can we bring?"

"An appetizer to nibble on while I grill would be good. How is the investigation going?"

"Which one do you want to hear about first?" Jeff asked. "I'm tugged in a couple of directions after the weekend."

"How about the one closest to being solved?" Scott asked.

I buckled my seatbelt for the ride back to Harmony. I knew what was coming.

"We found botulism in an opened food container in Pierre's condo today. That's where he must have gotten the toxin from. He didn't address it quickly enough and with the weakening from dehydration, it ended up killing him. Sad case. Especially for someone who works with food."

"So, what was the toxin found in?" Scott asked. "I hope others didn't catch it too?"

"Luckily, it wasn't something served at the Taste of Harmony. But, and please keep this between us, it came from a Country Kitchen Catering jar."

"My ex-wife's catering business?" Scott asked. "Oh man. That's hard to hear."

"Pierre asked her for some product samples for possible use in the Timbers Grill. We found the remnants in his trash can and the health inspector said it tested positive for the bacteria."

"Guess that closes that case. Hope it doesn't affect Patti's business negatively," Kay said.

"Me too, but it's bound to hurt her reputation. I was with Jeff when he got the news, so I wanted to be the one to tell her. She's taking it pretty hard. It's serious, of course, but I know she's very careful with her food handling," I said.

Scott and I were in the rear seat. He put his arm on the seat back behind me, giving my shoulder a squeeze. I almost shared my thoughts about the call I'd made this afternoon, but I had to be patient.

"And Mitch? You don't have a likely suspect for his murder?"

"I have several and I'm going through them trying to confirm alibis."

"The wife first. Always check the spouse," Kay said. "Isn't that the classic case?"

"Faye went home after the concert. But alone. So not a clear alibi for her."

"Didn't she find it strange her husband didn't come home on a Saturday night?" Kay asked.

"Not unusual for her husband. He has that small cabin cruiser in the harbor and has slept there, according to her."

"Alone?" Kay asked. "Or is that a dumb question?"

"If you knew Mitch, it would be. He always thought himself quite the ladies' man. But any luster he had is wearing thin with age. There was evidence he was expecting company on the boat that night. I have a witness who saw someone in the vicinity of his boat and within the time frame of his death."

"And was that a man or a woman?"

"By clothing and frame size, the witness leaned toward it being a woman," Jeff said. "But I have to wonder if a slight woman would have the strength to plunge that weapon into him. Mitch's body may have softened with age, but he was still strong. He could have easily fought a smaller adversary off."

Scott had another question. "Who else are you looking into?"

"I questioned Miguel from the steakhouse."

"Really? Why would he do that?" Kay asked.

"Did you see the argument they had? Dolly's tent was right next to his, and Vivian told me about a very confrontational scene she'd witnessed. I think it's a stretch that he had anything to do with it. Plus, after cleanup, he rode back to Madison with his employees so pretty tight alibi there."

"Mitch had enemies from his work dealings," I said. "But that opens up so many. Have you gotten to some of those yet? You said MJ was going to get some names for you."

"He did. I'm still checking those out."

"What about MJ?" Scott asked. "I've witnessed how Mitch treated his own son. He could be a mean man. Jackie and I saw how upset Murph got when Mitch taunted Ginger. MJ steered his dad away from us. But could he be at a breaking point? Or, like Kay said, Faye was there, and Mitch said some nasty things about her too."

"Both of them are on my radar. But I'm still waiting for the autopsy. Doc is back in town and said he'd push the Greensville medical examiner to move it along. Hopefully, it'll show up on my desk in the morning."

"I know you've got to have an autopsy done," Scott said. "But isn't it obvious what killed him? You had to have noticed the spear in his chest."

Jeff managed a small laugh. "It's a skewer, not a spear. And of course, I noticed it. I also noticed there was no blood around the wound."

"I can confirm what he's saying," I said. "It shocked

me when he had the body loaded in the coroner's van for transport with the skewer still stuck in it. Jeff wanted the examiner to see the skewer as we found it."

"One reason there wouldn't have been blood released was if the heart was no longer pumping," Jeff said.

Scott gasped. "You're not thinking a poisoning like Pierre's? Do you think it was a poisonous spear?"

"Stop with the spear! But now that you say that…"

"Okay you two, enough sparring," I said, giving Scott's thigh a squeeze. "It's getting late and we're all getting punchy."

CHAPTER TWENTY-THREE

y first thought on waking the next morning was to find out if Stu's research efforts had found anything I could use. The second was that Libby needed to be let outside. "Sorry girl. I've been ignoring you, haven't I? I'm making my way to the coffee shop, and I'll bet Grace has one of her baked doggie treats waiting for you."

After confirming that Todd didn't need me for anything today, I headed out. My first stop was the office of our own local paper, the Harmony Happenings. A print edition still went out twice a week, but the online version was growing in popularity. Stu greeted me with an offer I had a hard time refusing. My favorite maple-frosted donut and some fresh coffee. "I'm making my way to Grace and Dermot's because of this little one. She loves the doggy treats Grace bakes for our furry families. I will have to pass on your kind offer. Any news for me?

"No. Honestly, I haven't gotten to spend much time on it yet. But I'll let you know something today. Now that Tuesday's edition is out, I can tend to some other items. Like your research and interviewing Jeff about how his murder investigations are going."

"Okay, thanks. I'll check with you later."

"Jackie, since you're going to Murphy's, why not see if Dermot's brother Paddy is still there? He was chief of police during the period you were asking about. He might remember something in line with what you're searching for."

"Excellent idea, Stu. I will do that."

Before I made it to Murphy's, I saw Kim through the windows of the empty storefront connected to the coffee shop. She was with Ginger. They must be working on plans for her new bookstore.

"Good morning, ladies. Is this where the magic is going to happen?"

Grace flung her arms up. "Welcome to the Book Nook! Please step in." She pointed to the common wall. "Note our neighbor the delightful and delectable Murphy's Coffee Shop and Bakery right through that lovely open archway. Now you can enjoy both stores without leaving!"

"I can see it now," I said.

Ginger took a bow as Kim continued. "Isn't this exciting Jackie? We're having the structure checked to see if we can open the wall through to the coffee shop. Grace and Dermot own this entire building, and they are going to lease this half to Ginger. It's perfect. Coffee and cookies and books!"

"Please, this way." Grace ushered me to the corner near the window. "Here is our wine bar available for evening book clubs." She walked further along the wall, tapping against it with each step. Hearing a hollow sound, she said, "Here is our inviting fireplace. It says come in out of the cold and sit awhile."

Kim's hips wiggled with excitement. "We discovered it after Dermot pointed out the brick chimney outside. This place has been vacant since the children's store went out. They'd boarded over the fireplace. Can you believe it? It will feature a welcoming seating area to get toasty warm as winter storms rage outside."

"Oh, and we'll invite authors to come for book signings," Ginger exclaimed.

"Wow, this will be perfect for your store. It'll be a big draw for you to have the coffee shop and the bookstore connected. And a perfect addition to Harmony's downtown area."

"MJ is on his way over to check out some construction things for me. I really can't believe this is happening. It's been a dream of mine since I was a little girl. That and being a librarian, which sadly I will have to give up."

"I agree with you, Jackie," Kim said. "It's perfect for our village. We've been looking at other properties for months. When the kids' store that was leasing from the Murphy's moved out, bam! I got on it immediately. I couldn't let it slip away. Patti's bringing over information we'll need to get permitted to do the changes to the building. Jackie, is something wrong?"

I couldn't tell Kim what they had discovered in Pierre's condo yesterday. She'd be all on it with Patti when she got here. In fact, I decided avoidance of the entire situation was the best policy for now. "Nothing Kim. I just realized I needed to get going. Congratulations on the new business and I wish you all the best!"

By the time Patti walked by from her offices at the Village Administration Building, Libby and I were safely tucked away in a corner of the coffee shop. She looked pretty glum. Had Jeff already heard bad news from the health department?

"Who are you hiding from, lass?"

"Certainly not you, Paddy Murphy. Please pull up a seat. You are just the person I was looking for."

"Now why would that be?" Paddy set his own coffee cup down on the small round table and pulled a chair over that creaked as he sat down.

With his disarming Irish grin Paddy said, "I know this is part of the antique, eclectic, comfy look Grace is going after, but I've broken one of her chairs before and I hope it's not happening again." He wiggled slowly back and forth. "It's holding for now. But speak quickly because I don't know if I'll be dropping below the table in a pile of old wooden spindles and rails soon."

I choked on the coffee I'd just sipped. Paddy reached over to pat me on the back, and Libby's eyebrows bent up and down inquisitively.

"There now. I didn't know I had such an effect on people," Paddy said with a laugh.

Finally getting my voice back, I said, "It was just the visual of you crashing down and slipping out of sight that hit me."

"But back to the question you had for me."

"It has to do with the murder that happened."

"The body they found on the path?"

"Yes."

Our conversation was interrupted when Kim came

running through the front door of the coffee shop. "Have you heard?"

"MJ called and said he couldn't meet us here because his mother just got the news. Mitch died of a heart attack! His autopsy came in and he had a heart attack. Myocardial infarction. Is that the word? I can't believe this. Here we all thought it was murder by skewer."

All conversation in the coffee shop stopped, except for Kim, who had more information from MJ and continued with her news.

"The skewer stuck in him did not come anywhere close to killing him. Autopsy came back. He died of a heart attack. Oh wait, I said that already. But he didn't die from the skewer. It was just in him. It didn't kill him. So, he wasn't murdered. He died from natural causes."

She paused. Perplexed. "But why did he have that thing stuck in his chest?"

She looked at the eyes staring at her, as though for an answer. With a quick nod of her head and an adjustment of her shoulders, she said, "I should get back to Ginger. I just thought you all might want to know we didn't have another murder in Harmony. Especially you, Jackie."

"Me? Why me?"

Paddy's expression was priceless. "Who was that? I noticed her at the Taste. Kicks up her heels right smartly."

"Our local realtor extraordinaire, Kim Walters. She's often the bearer of news. And in this case, I guess you'd call it good news."

"Why did she say especially for you?"

"Probably because of what you heard about me. Since I returned to live in Harmony, the village has witnessed an unusually high number of murders. She directed her remark to that. Like yay! Jackie didn't find another murdered body."

"The legend of Jinxing Jackie takes a blow?" Paddy teased.

"Does this mean Jeff will set aside the investigation?" I crossed my fingers under the table that now, if this news was true, I could let go of the very uncomfortable thoughts I'd been having.

Paddy answered. "Absolutely not. He didn't stab himself with the skewer. Someone did that. Maybe he had the heart attack after it or during it. Despite that, the deed was done by someone who meant him ill. The perpetrator could be charged with attempted murder. Or mutilation of a corpse." He shook his head and took a sip of coffee, absently resting his hand on Libby's head.

Once again, Kim's reappearance interrupted us. "They stabbed Mitch after he died! Who on earth would do that? What kind of sick person would kill a man when he's down? I mean, skewer him when he's down? What skewered perspective on life do you have to have to skewer a dead person? I'm not trying to be funny," Kim said, getting confused by her own rush of words. "He may have been an unpleasant person, but that doesn't give anyone the right to skewer him!" Kim clapped her hand over her mouth and again walked out the front door.

"Was that her last appearance? She got to a good point, but in a very roundabout way," Paddy said. "Who sticks a skewer in a dead man?"

"Someone with a skewered perspective?"

"Don't you start too," Paddy said with a smile.

Wanda had used the word perspective when she explained how she didn't want to talk about Mitch and whatever had happened between them. Perspective. Such an interesting word in our complex world.

After Paddy explained they could still charge the person holding the skewer with a crime, I knew I had to clear this up. If Wanda wouldn't tell me, maybe someone else could.

Paddy said he'd think about what I asked. "I have a couple of thoughts about that. Tell me, are you asking for a friend?"

"I am. It's important."

"Is your friend in trouble?"

"She might be."

"I'm meeting with Orin at the Stone Mill right now. He's going to give me some pub ideas and I wouldn't mind sampling some of his brews. Thinkin' I might set up a brewery in the place back in Florida. Small though, no competition for the Guinness Brewery."

I suggested he try my favorite, the Pulp Man Red Ale.

"Cute name. What does it mean?"

"The building was a paper mill, and that was one of the work positions. Pulp men."

He nodded. "I'll try it. After that meeting, I'll get thinkin' about those times you spoke of."

Just as Paddy walked out the door, Patti waltzed in.

Her attitude was all sunshine and butterflies. She practically floated across the room to give me a hug.

"Jackie, you had to be the first one to share my good news with. Jeff called and told me that my vegetables were not the source of the toxins that killed Pierre. It was a false positive. Can you believe it?"

"That's wonderful, Patti. I'm so happy for you. What does Jeff think caused the infection?"

"Jeff said the search would continue, but that now the possibility of it coming in through an open wound is on the table. Can you believe they tested bandaging found in the garbage? It shows signs of having toxins on it. How those nasty bacteria got on it, who knows? But as for me, I'm free! Free of worry that I'm mishandling the food I love to work with. Free of thinking I could have caused someone's death. Gives me a whole new perspective on life."

That word again. This news meant something much different to me than it did to Patti. Our perspectives were different. And I had to get to Jeff and let him know my thoughts on who might have wanted to see Pierre suffer.

It took over half an hour with Jeff to go over my thoughts about Pierre's wound and how the botulism toxin ended up in it. He took careful notes, and I felt he was understanding and respecting my take on what might have happened Friday night. I shared the outcome of the call I'd made. "I think this poisoning was intentional, though the perpetrator might not have thought it could cause death. She was used to seeing it being injected into people without adverse side effects."

"Let me pull together a few things here on my end. I'll put a call into Doc and the health inspector. This could prove to be the break in the case. I'll check with the staff at the doctor's office and confirm what you discovered. Now find me the character who stabbed a man when he was down and out, and I'll be eternally grateful to you. I admit I'm stumped with that one."

"Thanks, Jeff. I'm glad you don't think my idea is crazy."

CHAPTER TWENTY-FIVE

*B*ack at the studio, Mandy was at work changing the window exhibit.

"I didn't think you'd be in today," I said as I released Libby from her leash, and she ran up to her buddy. Mandy reached in her pocket for the treat Libby knew would be there. Libby went to lie down by baby Ty asleep in his carrier on the floor and began crunching on her treat.

"Libby loves him, even knowing he'll wake up and begin tugging at her ears," Mandy said. "Thought I'd catch up around here. The photographer from Door County that you're featuring next called and asked if she could bring her things down tomorrow and I said sure. But I realized I needed to pull all this out first."

"Her work is stunning. Especially the lavender fields.

I've never taken the ferry to Washington Island way up at the northern end of the peninsula, but now I want to see the lavender in bloom."

Mandy closed her eyes and took in a deep breath. "Oh, I can almost smell those fields now! Patti gave Matt and I an adult night away a few weeks ago, treating us to an overnight at Kay's. She has lavender sachets on the pillows at her B&B and it's heavenly."

"I'll bet Patti's gift included an overnight for Ty with her and Charlie. Say, have you heard the health inspector has cleared her food?"

"I did. She was so relieved. I heard you were a part of that discovery."

"In a roundabout way," I said.

"Do they have any lead on the source of botulism?"

"Jeff is going to be talking with someone today about another possible way the toxins got into Pierre. Mandy, did you like working with the group from the Hills?"

"I absolutely loved it. They are so fun. Joking and kidding with each other, sharing their stories about the photographs. And always chatter about neighbors, friends, fellow Hills residents."

"I'll bet they were sad about Pierre's death. I think they all enjoyed his company."

"I suppose they would be. Sounded like he was their pseudo counselor on life in a luxury resort in Wisconsin. Haha. Life can be rough. They'd poke fun at themselves about the trials and tribulations they had to endure."

This might be my chance to talk to the housewives and get more proof for Jeff. "Would you like me to take these things up to the Hills for you?"

"Thanks, but Ava is coming to pick them up. She should have been here by now, though." Mandy glanced at her watch.

Ty began to cry, and Libby started to whine. I offered to warm Ty's bottle and feed the hungry little guy, so Mandy could finish taking down and packing up the exhibit. And now I'd be here to talk to Ava.

"I'd appreciate that," Mandy said, lifting Ty up out of his carrier. "Here you go, Grandma."

"Not officially yet."

"But I'm going to let him associate your face with that word. So when the wedding happens it will automatically roll off his tongue. Have you set a date yet?"

"We're making more decisions each day. In fact, tomorrow I'm going out to the Harmony House Museum. We've decided we'd like to hold it there. It was where our attraction to each other grew."

"That's sweet," Todd said as he came out of the back room brushing dust off his shirt. "I know you're going to expand our space up into your apartment when you move in with Scott. The sooner the better, we're busting at the seams here. Why not just do it now and we could start work on the remodeling?"

"How did you know those were my plans?"

"Jackie, think about it. Remember, this is a small town and word gets around."

So true. Thinking back, I had mentioned it to Scott. Then there was that time I asked Aunt Ruth her opinion about it. Wanda and Val asked me what I planned to do with the upstairs apartment, and we tossed around ideas. Things would be so different for me when that happened.

The jingling of the bell above the front door announced the arrival of Olivia and Kayla.

But no Ava.

CHAPTER TWENTY-SIX

"Ava sends her apologies," Olivia said. "So here we are instead! She called just a couple of minutes ago to ask us to stop in here and pick up the photography work displayed in your window. She caught us on our way into town for some of Grace's strawberry-rhubarb muffins."

"Maybe she just heard about Chef Pierre's passing," Mandy suggested. "I knew him from some of the restaurant menu and promotional things he hired me to photograph. It was a shock for everyone."

"No, she was the first one to know because the hospital notified her of his death. I'm not sure how she got on his emergency form," Olivia said.

"Well…" Kayla rolled her eyes and kiss-kissed her lips. "She was a little closer to him than the rest of us."

This is what I had guessed at. It was true.

"When was the last time you saw him?" I asked.

"Briefly on Saturday," Kayla said. "We witnessed his getting upset with that handsome Brazilian Miguel. Then he left early."

"What was that about, anyway?" Olivia said. "I never heard what they argued about."

"Miguel didn't care for the Timbers gazpacho. Pierre noticed him toss the rest of it in the trash. Pierre got on his high horse. Miguel was ragging on him about it. Pierre can be pompous at times and Miguel played him."

That fit. Miguel was the one who told us that Peter was Pierre's real name. There was some history there.

"Could the gazpacho have contained the toxin? I mean, if it tasted off, and it was in the Timbers booth," Todd asked.

"No, it was on the health inspector's list of what he cleared," I said.

"Anyway, Friday was the last time we actually talked with Pierre. He seemed in good spirits but turned in early to rest up for Saturday."

"Where was that?"

"At the bar in Timbers. We were all there. Junene and Ava had left early because their husbands were going to be in town that night. Then Pierre left shortly after. We gals had made plans to meet at the Taste on Saturday.

The rest of the guys got in early Saturday morning to meet up for golf."

Had I been mistaken in what I heard Phoebe say about Ava's husband staying behind to work on Saturday? No, Ava must have lied to her friends that he was going to be in Harmony. This fit perfectly. She must have thought she would sneak away to spend the night with Pierre.

One more test to confirm. "Do your husbands get along?"

"They get along great. Two are doctors, one is a lawyer, one is retired, and one runs some sort of family business. What's not to get along? And they all have beautiful, loving, over the top gorgeous wives!" Olivia said.

Mandy added, "With talent!"

"Say, what's happening with that other guy's death?" Kayla asked.

"It's still being investigated," I said. "But he died of a heart attack, not a stabbing."

"Whew. The way Miguel was acting toward him, it had crossed my mind that they could have gotten into an altercation too. That Miguel is trouble." Kayla drew out the last word.

"Oh really? Why is that?" I asked. "I thought he was a nice enough guy."

Olivia winked. "I think she meant good trouble for women and a jealous trouble for men. Testosterone kicking in trouble."

"Someone else mentioned that about him." I remembered Dolly's comment at the diner. She nailed it.

"Still, someone stabbed him," Todd said.

"That's true, but it changes things knowing the skewering didn't kill him." Kayla picked up one of the boxes.

"In the end, he got the wrong end of the skewer." Olivia laughed and picked up a second box.

Paddy was just entering and held the door open for Kayla and Olivia. "What's so funny?"

"A word," Mandy said with a grin.

"Here, let me help you with these," Paddy offered. "The rest go out in their car?"

I nodded, and he grabbed two of the boxes leaning against the wall. Within minutes, Kayla and Olivia were driving off.

Mandy explained what we'd been laughing about. When she used the term Real Housewives of The Hills, Paddy's quizzical expression led her to give an explanation. "The first Real Housewives television show was about a group of married women who lived in Orange County, California. There are like maybe ten more now...in Miami, New Jersey, Beverly Hills and other places. These aren't what you might think of as typical housewives. They usually have money to throw around and a nanny to help with the kiddos." She took Ty from me and put him back in his car seat. "I could use one of those," she continued with a soft cooing for her baby.

After she left, Paddy asked me to join him on the outside bench for a moment. He wanted to clarify a few things about what we'd discussed earlier.

CHAPTER TWENTY-SEVEN

"Jackie, I put some thoughts together about what we were discussing at the coffee shop earlier. You asked me if I remembered cases involving Mitch Carter back when you were teenagers."

"And…" I said.

"I do. You were right to believe he was involved in things that would have not made the papers. His father, Big Dan, was notorious for getting his son out of trouble. But you knew that, didn't you, Jackie?"

"I did. This is what I was asking Stu to research in the Harmony Happenings archives. But the police blotter they published then would not have printed names for juvenile offenses. As I said, I was looking for those cases that were never even reported."

"Where should I start?" Paddy closed his eyes and rubbed his forehead. "This hurts to admit, but I should have fought harder to convince witnesses to come forward, or injured parties to press charges. But times were different then. I guess we all thought kids would be kids and that their parents would handle discipline without the legal system getting involved. And most of the time, that worked."

"Could you run a few past me? I really need to figure out if any of them involved my friend."

"Do you think she might have been involved with what happened to Mitch?" Paddy asked.

"I've asked myself that question hundreds of times these past few days. With the murder of our high school friend and Mitch becoming one suspect, I realized my friend was concealing something that involved Mitch."

"Can't you ask her what happened?"

"She still won't talk about it. And Paddy, I'm afraid of what she might have done."

"Maybe you don't want to know either," Paddy suggested. "I mean, the guy died of a heart attack. Whoever stabbed him didn't kill him. If she wants to keep her secret, why stir things up for her? Those are not the words of a law enforcement officer, but of an old man aware of the ways of the world."

He had a point. Was I asking for trouble? Would my curiosity about the past help? Or would it only muddy the waters even more? I know I didn't want to lose a dear friend. But getting the information didn't mean I had to use it, or would that become an obstruction of justice? I had to learn more.

He told me about several cases involving Mitch during his teen years. The boating accident I already knew about. Assault and instigating fights. Several underage drinking episodes. Leaving the scene of an accident.

"The paper's editor at that time owed Big Dan. Enough so even the charge against his son would not show up on the police blotter. Dan had that much influence. And I let him get away with it. There could have been other charges in the county's jurisdiction. I think there was even a state case I checked into at one point."

"How frustrating for you," I told Paddy.

He nodded. "But if the person who stabbed Mitch is someone he injured long ago, it sure was carried around inside them for a long time."

Paddy's words echoed in my head. Was he right? Resentment. Anger. Retribution. Eye for an eye. Two wrongs don't make a right. They all bounced around in my brain.

"Beyond that," I said. "Could I ask you a couple of questions? The fight situation. Do you remember who was involved and hurt by Mitch?"

"Yeah, a kid from out of town. Happened after a football game at the high school. Mitch risked suspension because he started it, but the kid refused to press charges. Don't remember his name, but he lived two counties over."

"The assault case. What kind of assault?"

Paddy hesitated. "This was a bit more delicate. It was a sexual assault, Jackie."

I sagged against the bench. Oh, poor Wanda. So that's it. That's why she would never talk about it. Even to her closest friends. To carry something like that for all these years. No wonder she snapped when she heard Mitch talking about Ginger in such a nasty way. I was so wrapped up in my thoughts that I had a delayed reaction to his words that followed. Did he say the victim was dead?

"Who passed on?"

"The girl he assaulted," Paddy repeated patiently. "I heard she'd married and had children, so by all appearances she worked through things and did okay, but I know her uncle and he mentioned she passed away a few years ago."

"Wait, I don't understand. I thought…" I had to clear

my head and let the knowledge that Wanda wasn't the assault victim sink in.

"The girl's parents reported it to me. They were with me when I spoke to their daughter, but she wouldn't say anything more. I could see that she was embarrassed and ashamed. I'm not sure how her parents even got the information out of her to begin with."

"Was a rape kit done?"

"No, there wasn't a standardized protocol for collection of evidence, nor for preserving it at that time. The victim was dead set against anyone else finding out what Mitch had done to her. She said it wasn't a rape. She blamed herself for what happened. Not uncommon."

"You're right. I remember the women's movement was just gaining steam and growing up in a small town, reputations could be ruined on innuendo alone. Would I have known the girl?"

"You could of. Her name was Sandy Schuster. I think she was probably your age. Is this the crime you were hunting for?"

"Could be. I remember two girls with the name Sandy. Let me talk to my friend and see if there is a connection."

"Okay, but please keep it confidential. Even after all these years, it would be hard on her parents. Her father is still alive and I'm certain would not like to relive what happened to his daughter."

"Will do, and thanks Paddy. Where are you headed to now?"

"Thought I'd have a visit with Shorty. I used to join in the cribbage games a few afternoons over the years. His niece was the victim."

s soon as Paddy left, I thought about Sandy. I knew who he meant. Sandy Schuster. A beautiful girl. Book smart, but even in high school, she seemed naïve. So, Mitch had assaulted her. I could understand the explanation Paddy had just shared. It would have made complete sense. And even if she'd agreed to let the law handle it, it would have been a *he said she said*. What havoc Mitch Carter created in his lifetime. How many other crimes was he not brought to justice over?

Wanda could very well have known about it when it happened. She and Sandy had classes together and lived near each other in the Flats. She's not strong enough to drive a skewer into a large man's chest and kill him. But those were my thoughts before the autopsy. Could she have snapped, seeing Mitch's behavior at the festival Saturday evening? Did she finally snap and vent all the rage that had built up in her over the years?

No. I won't accept it. I can't accept it to be true. It just can't. I decided to check in with Val and see if she knew anymore about Sandy and Wanda's friendship.

Lucky for me, Wanda was in Val's beauty salon, probably making up for that missed Monday appointment. Through the front window I saw Val shaking out the pink cape and Wanda standing and brushing off her slacks as she looked in the mirror, turning her head from side to side. She caught sight of me in the reflection and smiled as she waved.

I took three deep breaths and joined Val and Wanda inside the Cut-n-Curl where another customer waited her turn.

"Hey, Jackie. Like the new do Val gave me? I was ready for something different, a summery cut."

"Looks great on you, Wanda. What are you up to now?" I had to take this chance to talk to her. We three couldn't talk in front of the waiting customer, so I would have to have this conversation with only Wanda. If I got to tell her what Paddy had shared with me, it might mean she'd open up. "I'm heading out for a walk on the Mary-Go-Round trail. Like to tag along?"

"Good idea. Let me just settle up with Val first."

Soon Libby, Wanda, and I were walking on the trail along the river east toward the Shady Pines retirement home.

"Remember when we discovered the story behind this trail's name?" I asked. "About how Mary Bell, torn up over her husband's indiscretions with my mother, took to walking to comfort herself?"

"I sure do. You've made your peace with that entire situation, haven't you?"

"I guess you could say that. It was the biggest shock of my life, but it also brought a half-sister and a niece into my life."

"I don't know why Mary didn't leave Judge Bell, instead of spending all her time hiking circles around Harmony. Good way to walk off angry energy."

"Divorce wasn't a simple thing then. And I suppose it never is. Remember, my mom and dad stayed together too. Times were different, weren't they Wanda?"

"Sure were." Wanda said softly, looking down at the trail as we walked.

"Did you know we just passed the spot where we found Mitch's body?"

Wanda turned to look back. "I try not to think about it. He was an unkind man. Have they found out who stabbed him?"

Was she giving me an opening? "Didn't you hear? He died of a heart attack."

"Val said something like that. Even so, someone must have wanted to kill him. You don't jam a long deadly skewer in a person's chest just to get his attention."

Time to push harder, I told myself. I knew where I'd start. "Rocco saw someone by Mitch's boat close to the time of the murder."

Wanda remained quiet.

I pushed. "Who do you think that might have been?"

"How would I possibly know that?" Wanda said in a cutting tone.

"The figure seemed to be a woman. She had a hood up covering her face, so he didn't get a close look. She had on light colored pants."

Wanda stopped and looked me right in my eye, staring, her eyes burrowing into me.

"You wore white jeans and a hooded sweater Saturday night."

The next words flew out of her mouth. "I can't believe you are accusing me of being on Mitch's boat. I hate the man."

"It's only a matter of time before Jeff calls you in, Wanda. Were you on his boat waiting to attack him?"

Wanda stormed off back down the trail toward the village green. I ran to catch up with her, calling out.

"Wait. Talk with me. You knew about Sandy, didn't you?"

That stopped her in her tracks. With her back still toward me, I watched her shoulders tremble. I reached out and gently directed her toward a bench on the trail. We both sat. I looked out over the river while Wanda's eyes remained downcast.

The first words she spoke were barely audible. "It was me."

I reached for her hand.

"Why were you there?"

"I didn't want him to die, Jackie. I just wanted him to know how it felt. To feel what Sandy felt. I swear that's all."

"Tell me what you knew about her assault."

"It was a party somewhere. A lot of us from school were there. Keith was around that night too. I remember when we walked in on Mitch and Sandy. She had a horrible, dazed look in her eyes. Later Keith learned that Mitch had slipped something into her drink."

"Was he raping her?"

Wanda shook her head. "No, they both were clothed. Mitch had his hands all over Sandy's disheveled clothes. He jerked them back when he saw us." Wanda gasped, "Jackie, I was afraid he would have gone much further. It was awful. Sandy was so sweet. An innocent. He was taking advantage of her. She could barely stand, but Keith and I got her out of that room."

"And she didn't press charges?"

"Right. It mortified Sandy that she'd gotten herself into that position. Like you said, times were different."

"But what were you going to do to Mitch? What could possibly have been going through your mind by waiting for him on the boat?"

"I acted stupidly," Wanda said. "I thought I'd put some of my old sleeping pills, from the days after John died, in Mitch's drinks on the boat so he would feel woozy and off kilter like Sandy had. It was just dumb, but I got the angriest I've ever been when I saw him drunk and picking on Ginger. When the thing happened to Sandy, I should have done more. I finally struck out in the only way I could think of. Not kill him, but just let him know what it felt like to be helpless."

"How did you know what he'd drink? Did he know you were waiting for him?"

"I played Mitch. It was easy. He was always so full of himself. He'd been a handsome man once, but his features had coarsened, and some women still find that attractive. But my perspective on what a crude man he was strengthened my resolve to drug him. What a wimp I turned out to be. When the time we'd agreed upon was getting close, I left his boat. I certainly didn't want anyone to see me, so I had that hood draped over my head. Some Mata Hari I was."

"But how did the skewer end up in your hands and in his chest?"

Wanda's eyes startled wide open. "I didn't do that! How could you even think that, Jackie? What kind of friend are you?"

"You said you left the boat and I...ah..."

"Thought I stabbed him? Really?"

"I'm sorry, but the way you were talking, I assumed you took the anger with you. That maybe you saw him lying on the ground after his heart attack..."

"And I picked up a handy dandy skewer? I didn't do it, but I saw who did. I saw what happened. Mitch was violently arguing with someone who held what looked like some sort of poker or large stick in his hands."

Oh my gosh, she could identify the murderer. Just like Jeff had been hoping. "Who was it?"

"I won't tell you."

"Do you want me to go with you to the police station and talk to Jeff?"

"Not really. I could be wrong."

I felt her back tracking now.

Wanda chuckled. Not what I expected at this moment. "Now Val won't have to do something awful to

Mitch and Chris won't have to bail her out. I'll talk to Jeff later, but I can't turn the man in. Not just yet."

"You could tell Jeff you saw them arguing. That this mystery man was being threatened by Mitch and was just defending himself."

Wanda seemed to consider my suggestion, then said, "Jackie, how would you have handled it? The thing Keith and I knew about? Would you have done it differently than we did? Than Sandy did? Look, let me think about how much to tell Jeff."

anda had a good point. But that still left the fact that someone stabbed Mitch. Are we back to his wife or a work associate? Take *we* out of that sentence, Jackie, you now know Wanda didn't do it, so step back and let Jeff figure it out. You can rest your curiosity now that both Patti and Wanda are in the clear.

But my heart sank as I watched Paddy stick his head out of the door to Shorty's bar and call me over, inviting me to enter the cool, dark place. Say thanks, but no thanks. I had a sinking feeling this was about Mitch. I wanted to be done with it all.

"This won't be easy," Paddy said as I pushed past him. "But please come in and listen with me. I think you deserve to understand what happened, since it involves people and times you were a part of."

Shorty stood behind the bar. I waved off his offer of beer because I was emotionally exhausted. I'd listen to what Paddy said, then leave.

But it was Shorty who spoke first. "Paddy told me you're worried about your friend who, how shall I put it, had a strong dislike for Mitch Carter. Do you mean Wanda?"

"I did, but how did you know that?"

"Because the victim of that assault, Sandy, was my niece." Shorty said. "And at the time, Sandy's mother and father shared details with me, including how Keith and Wanda walked in on the attack. I'm sorry you've been thinking Wanda was involved with what happened to Mitch."

"I appreciate you saying that, but it still leaves us without the person who stabbed him." I watched the knowing look exchanged between Shorty and Paddy. "Wait, this isn't just about me worrying about my friend, is it? You know more, don't you? Now that you've got me in here and it's 5 o'clock somewhere, I'll buy us a round while you two spill what you know."

"Sounds like a good plan, Jackie."

Shorty pulled a Pulp Man Red Ale draft for me, and

Paddy chose a Bud Light, patting his tummy. "Retirement has put some pounds on me."

"Just a soda for me, as I have some important business to attend to shortly and it's best to be done completely sober," Shorty said. "Now, back to the story we wanted you to hear. My niece's assault was horrible. She wanted no one else to know about it. Paddy probably told you that earlier."

"Was it only Sandy's decision? Or did anyone else pressure her?"

"To my knowledge, it was her alone. I know sometimes parents wish to silence the truth, to hide the supposed shame brought on them by their children. But I can tell you unequivocally that both of them urged Sandy to press charges. After all, she had witnesses, and they could have taken a blood sample to prove someone had drugged her. They were ready to fight tooth and nail to make Mitch Carter accountable. Begrudgingly, her parents accepted her wish to keep the assault out of the hands of law enforcement."

Here Paddy took over. "I know this to be true. I was in on the private conversations. What surprised me at the time was that Dan Carter himself didn't step in to influence Sandy's decision like he'd done so often. Maybe even he knew Mitch had gone too far."

"But why are you telling me this now?"

"My brother has lived with this inner rage since then. I think the stress might have made his cancer worse. In fact, now cancer is taking his life. When his daughter passed away, I thought he'd let go of it and be able to put it to rest. Apparently, I was wrong."

"I'm confused. What does all this have anything to do with what happened to Mitch?"

"You were near us on Saturday night," Paddy said. "And heard and saw what I did. How rude and crude Mitch was. My opinion is that the scene made Stanley snap."

"Stanley? Who's that?"

"My brother. Stanley was there with friends from Shady Pines. I believe your Aunt Ruth was with them too. He is part of our cribbage crew."

"I remember some unfamiliar faces. One of them was Sandy's father? But what do you mean he snapped?"

"He went after Mitch."

Those four simple words took my breath away. Was Shorty telling me that Stanley, obviously an elderly man in poor health, had been the one to push the skewer into Mitch's chest? It seemed as unlikely as Wanda being able to do it.

"The possibility that Sta, in his condition, could have overpowered a stumbling drunk like Mitch, seemed far-fetched when Shorty first shared it with me," Paddy said.

"When Jeff learned Mitch had died of a heart attack, I could see that he might have fallen on the skewer Sta held."

"Now it's my turn to tell you something I just learned. Wanda witnessed the fight on the river path that night. And she recognized the man there but didn't want to say who it was. But now it all fits together. It was Stanley. Will you be telling the Chief about this?"

From behind me, a voice answered. "I will be the one to confess. No more secrets. Even though I didn't kill him, doesn't mean it wasn't on my mind."

"Sta, are you sure you're ready? You just had a treatment Monday, and that knocks you out for a couple of days," Shorty said.

"Gotta be done with it all. Whatever they want to do with me cannot be worse than the cancer I carry. I'm not long for this earth, but knowing that man is gone, I feel free. Want to walk over to the police station with me, brother?"

"You bet I do."

"Is it okay if I call Wanda? She wants to talk with Jeff too. Turns out she had a part in that night, only it didn't turn out as she planned it."

Sta smiled at me. "Of course. I only wish Keith Steele had lived to see this day. He and Wanda were ready to support my Sandy and turn Mitch in. They probably lived with the regret that no one held Mitch to account. So yes, for Wanda to be there would be a perfect ending. But what is her connection now?"

I took Sta's elbow and as we walked along past Parker Photography, Val's Cut-n-Curl, and Dolly's Diner, I explained what Wanda had tried to do. Sta's hearty laugh sounded good.

"Hey up there, you two," Paddy called out as he walked behind us with Shorty. "What's so funny? Share with us, why don't you."

Sta turned to speak to them. "Someone had my same idea, that Mitch needed to have his comeuppance. Wanda was always a spunky gal, but this story about her giving him a dose of his own medicine takes the cake!"

CHAPTER THIRTY

I used my cell phone to text Wanda that I had surprising news, and I was headed to the police station with some friends. Wanda quickly responded that she was just leaving the marina with Jeff and Murph. How about we meet at the village green?

Except for trampled grass, all signs of the weekend's Taste of Harmony were gone. And we would now clear up the final lingering mystery of the death that happened during the Taste.

I saw Wanda's shocked reaction when she saw who was with me. She walked up and embraced Sta, her eyes tearing up as they sat next to each other at a picnic table.

Before joining us at the table, Jeff sent Murph back to the station. "I'll have him write up what Wanda pointed us to. Hopefully, with her help, we're closer to finding out who stabbed Mitch. What was your surprise news?"

I cleared my throat. "Jeff, please feel free to speak in front of everyone here. They have something to share with you too. But first, what did you and Wanda find on the boat?"

Wanda told her story about the drinks she'd planned to spike with her sleeping aids to show Mitch what Sandy felt. Sta winced when she spoke those words.

"Are you charging her with anything?" Shorty asked.

"No. Because she came forward with what she'd done, I feel it is unnecessary to charge her. The only possibility now would be trespassing, but people are always letting themselves on to friend's boats here in the marina. I'd have a full plate if I started doing that." He shot Wanda a look. "You will have to work harder on a description of the person you saw fighting with Mitch, though."

"I've got a feeling I won't have to work hard at it at all," Wanda murmured, looking at Sta and squeezing his hand.

"She's right, Jeff, it was me who stood next to that vile person late Saturday night." Sta held his head up proudly, his stare fierce, without speaking another word.

Jeff took a deep breath and with a slow exhale,

absorbed what he'd just been told. "Well now, this puts a twist in my investigation."

Shorty took over the explanation for his brother. "It was before your time as Police Chief. When Wanda here was still in high school." He winked at Wanda. "Hmm, I forgot to report those fake ids you kids tried to manufacture and use."

Paddy chuckled. "Some things never change. But go on, Shorty."

"A sexual assault occurred. My brother Stanley's daughter Sandy was the victim of that assault."

"And did the perpetrator happen to be Mitch Carter?" Jeff asked.

"Correct. There were two witnesses who could testify to the truth of it. One of them has recently died. Keith Steele. The other is sitting next to Sta. Wanda and Keith walked in on Mitch assaulting Sandy and stopped him before he went even further."

"Date rape drug involved?" Jeff asked, looking pointedly at Wanda, who nodded.

"I'm beginning to understand what this powwow is about." With a huge sigh, Jeff pushed himself up from the table and paced with his hands behind his back.

"Bear with me while I let this new information sink in. Stop me if my assessment of what happened that evening is incorrect. There was a group of you gathered here on the village green to enjoy each other's company and the music from the band. Mitch Carter made an appearance and disrupted your peaceful evening. He left, but his conduct inflamed old angers. Wanda, somehow you contacted him to meet you at his boat, where you planned to have drinks spiked with sleeping pills. Sta, you left the gathering only to return later. You found an errant meat skewer and approached Mitch on his way to a rendezvous with Wanda. The skewer you held was for self-defense, since you obviously would have been on the bad side of a physical fight. An argument ensued. Mitch had a heart attack, and you held the skewer at such an angle that the now dying body fell into it. In alarm, you tried to heave it away, sending the body crashing backwards into the wild grasses along the path."

No one spoke.

"Since no one is protesting this synopsis, I will take it to be factual. As with the Wanda situation, I feel there are no appropriate charges to file against Mr. Schuster."

Sta collapsed, his head falling down into his arms where they rested on the table.

"Does anyone feel any further need to speak?" Jeff asked in an official tone.

Again, no one spoke.

"Well then, I'll return to the station to fill out the case

report and close the file." Jeff tipped his head to those of us seated at the picnic table. "Have a good evening, everyone."

Harmony businesses were closing for the day. Val locked the front door of her salon and walked toward our group. "How come I wasn't invited to this? Care to share what's going on?"

"You're off the hook on defending me," Wanda teased her.

"Oh yeah? Well, good. Tell me all about it later, friend. My hubby is grilling out for me tonight. Ribs and packets of potatoes, onion, and butter. My stomach is growling already."

"Enjoy. How about we all catch up on the weekend? I'm heading home to put my feet up and lose myself in a good cozy mystery book," Wanda said.

"I'm heading home to feed Libby. She's had a long day." Libby's ears perked up, and I felt a gentle tug on the leash. "I know, girl. Time we went home and got something in our tummies."

Shorty patted Sta on the shoulder. "Come on, brother, looks like my thirsty customers are trickling in. Started a new bartender last week and don't want to leave him alone with my evening rush."

Paddy stood. "I'm going too. Dermot and Grace will be waiting for me. My last meal in Harmony this visit."

We settled in on my little second-floor balcony after both of us finished eating, Libby curled contently at my feet as the streetlights turned on. I would miss sunrises and sunsets from my little south facing balcony when I moved to Scott's place. I wanted no further thoughts about the tragedies this week, only to sit and enjoy my tranquil evening view.

Things were getting back to normal.

CHAPTER THIRTY-ONE

Mandy had completed the display from the Door County photographer. Things felt freshened up in the studio and I was looking forward to a new uninterrupted day of work here with Mandy.

She chatted about how relieved her mother-in-law was to know none of her food items had been the culprit of Pierre's poisoning. I decided not to share with Mandy the things I'd told Jeff yesterday. I hoped I was wrong about where my thoughts took me, but if Jeff had confirmed things with the bandage test results and the calls he was going to make, the entire village would find out soon enough.

"I'm so happy for her," I said, settling in behind our store front computer. "I've been considering a few tweaks to our online store, like offering framing services for customers who buy prints."

"That sounds like a terrific idea," Mandy said.

"Think you could handle the business if it takes off?"

"Could I? You bet I could! I didn't want to suggest it myself, but it's been on my mind. Thank you for thinking of me."

We both looked up when the front doorbell jingled.

"Hi Junene. Your photographs are with Olivia and Kayla. They were in yesterday to pick up the displayed prints," Mandy said.

"That's not why I'm here. I'm on to the next thing. Could you display this poster for our upcoming golf tournament at the Driftless Course, please?"

"Of course, we'd be happy to." Mandy took the poster and grabbed some tape to put it in our front window.

"How did your game with Scott go on Tuesday?" Junene asked me.

"Actually, pretty well. Thanks so much for the pointers you gave me on Monday. It warmed me up enough to make all eighteen holes without totally embarrassing myself."

"Have you heard about Ava?"

I didn't want to add anything showing I had prior

knowledge about what I thought she was going to say. So I simply replied, "What about her?"

"She is being charged with poisoning Pierre." Junene shook her head in disbelief.

"What? Seriously?" I hated doing this fake ignorance but felt it would be better in the long run. Now if only Ava's husband didn't put two and two together and realize who made the call to him claiming to be a friend. I didn't think he would make the connection. I hoped not.

"I know. In some ways it's hard to believe," Junene paused, reconsidering. "But then, looking back, I can see how things fit. Did you know Pierre's real name was Peter?"

"Miguel at the Brazilian steakhouse mentioned it to me."

"I suppose he thought Pierre sounded more chef-like and professional than Peter. That it elevated him somehow."

"So, what did Ava do, if you don't mind me asking?"

"I'm not clear on that. But confidentially, I think she was getting caught up in a love triangle. No, more like a lust triangle. I suspected some shenanigans were going on between her and Pierre, but hey, we're all grownups. I told myself to mind my own business. But apparently, he was getting weary of her and toyed with advances from… Never mind, I'll just leave more names out of this. We really sound like a bunch of goofy bored house-wives, don't we?" Junene said with a laugh. "Maybe we should promote ourselves to the franchise that created those TV shows. The Midwest could use a bit of glitz occasionally. But seriously, much as we love her, what Ava did was awful."

"What did she do?" Mandy asked.

"Her husband is a dermatologist. A huge part of his practice includes doing Botox injections. Ava plotted to get some botulism cells or spores, whatever the heck the poison is called, into Pierre to make him sick. Then nurse Ava would swoop in and nurse him back to health. Voila, she would be in his good graces again."

"A little sick. Isn't it deadly?" Mandy asked.

Junene shook her head. "Nope."

"So, you've talked to her then?" I asked.

"No, her husband told us everything."

"Wow," Mandy said. "I can't believe she did that."

"She didn't plan on killing him. But she did…" Junene's fingers added air quotes to the next word. "Accidentally cut him while they were preparing some appetizers. Simple enough for nurse Ava to dress Pierre's wound with a bandage that held a smidge of the poison on it. She never imagined the infection would lead to death. Then Ava tried to use her husband as an alibi for where she was on Friday night, but your police chief had already spoken to his office staff, and they confirmed he stayed in town on Friday and worked Saturday, so her alibi fell apart."

"What will they do to her?" I asked, wincing at the truth I'd uncovered.

"I don't know the charges yet. She'll get a high-priced attorney and fight it, I'm sure. Such a shame it all came to this. Say, how is that other murder investigation going? The one with that crude, pompous guy we met at the Taste. This so called quiet little village keeps that cute Jeff Bridges lookalike Chief of Police busy."

Giving no hint of my involvement, I explained they solved the case just yesterday afternoon. "Turns out he died of a heart attack and the stabbing was accidental."

CHAPTER THIRTY-TWO

After Junene left, Mandy and I went back to going over some more ideas for our online store. I talked to her about the changes I was planning for the studio after I moved in with Scott.

"Cool. It would give me more room for storing the additional framing materials I'll need. Especially once the Christmas rush starts."

"Whoa, slow down. Not planning on starting it until after the wedding. But I definitely will take your and Todd's input on how to do this remodeling. Having the entire upper level available will free up space."

"So proper! The whole town knows you don't spend every night in your own place." Mandy's suggestive tone made me laugh.

"Is that so! Hopefully, the summer weather and

outdoor activities will give them something else to think about."

"How are the wedding plans going?"

"I've just begun getting serious about them. I almost gave my Chicago friends a heart attack when I began describing the red crushed velvet bridesmaid dresses and matching shoes I'd chosen for them."

Mandy burst out laughing. "Good one! You're not doing all the bridesmaid stuff, are you?"

"No, that's one thing I'm sure of. But I might do a few traditional sorts of things. It's still up in the air."

"I'll give you a suggestion. Talk to Kate Harper about seasonal flowers. Not only is it economical, but makes her job easier."

"Lesson learned from your own wedding?"

"Yes, ma'am it was," Mandy said. "And I love that you're using the Harmony House."

"Me too. What they've done with it since Eleanor left it to the Historical Society is impressive. I've been to a couple of events there and they have all the kinks worked out."

"Jackie, why don't you enjoy the rest of the day doing some wedding planning?" Mandy said. "Go check in with Kate at The Flower Girl, and maybe stroll through the Harmony House. It might inspire you!"

"I sure could use inspiration, especially on what to

wear. I'm usually confident in my fashion choices, and I have a few ideas, but nothing is rising to the top."

"How about extending your trip to Los Angeles for the premier of your sister's movie? I bet Beverly and Alli would love to take you shopping for your wedding dress."

"You know that's not a bad idea!" I said. "I'm disappointed the premier won't be here in Harmony but finding a wedding dress would make the trip even more special."

I left the studio walking on a cloud. Mandy was right about opening myself up to inspiration. It would feel magical if we did December, with snow on the ground and Christmas lights twinkling. I remembered how the Harmony House decorated itself last year with sparkling white lights strung all over, creating a fairyland atmosphere. It would be perfect.

My first stop was Kate's flower shop. She was excited to hear that I'd be having a Christmas wedding and had wonderful ideas. I learned that the Harmony House used her for their flower needs and when she described last year's holiday arrangements, I knew I was in the right hands. I left feeling comfortable with the things she suggested, now to just decide which ones I wanted to use.

Next, I drove up to the Harmony House and Museum. The mansion was still as stunning as ever. Inside I spoke with the new manager the Historical Society had hired to run not only the Museum and Nature Center but also to handle the social events. He pulled out all sorts of ideas. Certainly inspiring!

The next inspirational thing I did was head out for a walk on the Mary-Go-Round Trail. Doing this had so often helped me think about things that needed thinking and pondering on in the past. Libby and I found ourselves walking toward the Shady Pines waterfront area. There on the spacious lawn, those who did so much to build on their ancestors' work gathered. The backbone of the Historical Society!

Treats waited for Libby and conversation for me. Everyone wanted to hear about Sta and the backstory. Then the scandalous affair and subsequent poisoning that happened at The Hills was the next topic.

"Those new folk bringing trouble with them," Eunice grumbled.

Betty replied. "But it was the local folk from years ago involved with the Carter case."

"And your point is?" Eunice crabbed right back.

I scratched behind Libby's ears as she leaned contentedly against my legs.

Back to normal.

A perfect afternoon in Harmony.

he End

ABOUT THE AUTHOR

Here are a few ways to reach me…I'd love to stay connected!

Please <u>sign up for my monthly newsletter</u>. I'll share things about my life…both personal as Brenda Felber and professionally as my pen name Suzanne Bolden.
Like/follow Suzanne on her Facebook page

If you follow me on these two, you'll be automatically notified when new releases are available.
Bookbub
<u>Amazon Author Central</u>

Check out my website <u>www.suzannebolden.com</u>

Thank you for reading my books. If you enjoyed them, a review is much appreciated!

Katie Murphy Cozy Mystery Series

#1 Pour Decisions

#2 Pick Yar Poison

#3 Raising Spirits

#4 Auld Lang Stein

#5 A Wee Lepre-Con

#6 Paws for a Pint

7 The Elf Did It

#8 Matrimony and Malice

#9 Read Between the Lines